Esc

Cilla, lonely and isolated in her aunt's house, follows the suspicious Mr Bollow and finds herself plunged without warning into a hair-raising adventure. Captured and taken to the Devil's Gate, a narrowed mist-shrouded pass in the Welsh mountains, she meets new friends, Andy, Matt and Karen. Together they find themselves pitted against a gang of desperate criminals, who are determined to make a get-away with their loot.

This is Alan Evans's third thriller for children: the other two, *Running Scared* and *Kidnap!*, have also been published by Beavers.

ESCAPE
AT THE
DEVIL'S GATE

Alan Evans

Beaver Books

First published in 1978 by
Hodder and Stoughton Children's Books
47 Bedford Square,
London WC1B 3DP

This paperback edition published in 1980 by
The Hamlyn Publishing Group Limited
London · New York · Sydney · Toronto
Astronaut House, Feltham, Middlesex,
England
(Paperback Division: Hamlyn Paperbacks,
Banda House, Cambridge Grove,
Hammersmith, London W6 0LE)

Special Scholastic edition 1980
© Copyright Alan Evans 1978
ISBN 0 600 20304 2

Set, printed and bound in Great Britain by
Cox & Wyman Limited, Reading
Set in Intertype Baskerville

Contents

1 The storm — autumn

Bollow came on the first night of the storm that rampaged up and down the Welsh coast for three days. The lightning cracked so the village was lit brighter than noonday, thunder rattled the windows of the boarding-house and the wind shook it. The door crashed open and he came out of the dark on the wind of the storm as if he rode it. The aunt who opened to him had to set her shoulder to the door to close it.

He stood in the long hall, a barrel of a man in a black oilskin that glistened with the rain, and he talked with the aunt under the light.

The stairs were in shadow and so was the upstairs landing where Cilla crouched and watched through the rails. He had a wide, white face with small eyes that were never still and he smirked and flattered the aunt. She was won over and fussed around him but Cilla saw his face when the aunt's back was turned and the smile looked very like a sneer. He said he was a surveyor. The aunt was impressed but Cilla did not believe him.

Cilla was as much a stranger as he. She was small and pale with a mane of blonde hair, and lonely. She had come to live with the aunt while her parents were away but she knew that the aunt did not want her. The storm

and flooded roads stopped the school bus. At school she
might have made friends but she doubted it because she
knew she did not make friends easily.

The storm kept them all prisoner but on the third day
the wind eased and the rain changed from a downpour
into a drizzle with occasional sweeping showers. Bollow
had come in a landrover and on that third day he drove
out.

It was a small village, just one street of houses running
down the hill from her aunt's house. Cilla marked the
direction he took, heading south down the street and out
along the coast road. She followed on foot without much
hope because he might have gone twenty kilometres or
thirty or more – but she was quit of the house and grateful
for that. The village was left behind her and behind that
was farming land. To her left beyond a ditch and a low
hedge lay the coastal flats, clothed with meagre turf, and
beyond the flats lifted the distant mountains. To her right
lay the sea.

As she trudged down the road with the wind thrusting
at her and the rain on her face she saw the theodolite on its
tripod, visible over the low hedge and only a few metres
from it. At sight of the theodolite she took cover in the
hedge and looked for Bollow. There was a clump of
bushes near the road and the landrover was nosed into it.

Where was Bollow?

Then she saw him, far down the field and pacing across
it from the road.

He hammered a stake into the turf then paced back up
the field until he was level with the landrover. There he
knelt to hammer in another stake. When he rose he
stretched and looked around as a man who rested briefly
in his labour, but his eyes scanned the road and the plain

all around, and Cilla huddled down into her cover before
those searching eyes came to her. So he was watching to
see if he was watched. Her breath came faster. When she
raised her head again he was walking back and forth
across the field, lifting rocks and loading them into the
rear of the landrover. When he had a full load he drove to
the hedge and dumped the rocks in a pile. He paused
again while his eyes swept over the ground around him,
then he drove back into the field and started collecting
rocks once more.

So it went on. He worked and watched, worked and
watched until he reached the far end of the field and the
first stake. Cilla crouched behind the hedge, straddling
the ditch that ran like a small stream. He unloaded the
rocks, looked round once more, then climbed into the
landrover and turned it towards the hedge.

She had not noticed the bridge till then because it was
no more than two short baulks of timber wedged across
the ditch at a gap in the hedge. There was no time to run
and nowhere to run to. The landrover nosed through the
gap, dipped and rose as it crossed the timbers then acceler-
ated up the road. Cilla saw none of it because she was flat
in the ditch with the stream running under her and
around her.

The sound of the engine died away and she crawled out
of the ditch. She was wet through and her feet squelched
in her boots as she started back up the road. Bollow had
not seen her and she had found out *where* he was up to
whatever it was he was up to. One thing was certain:
Bollow was *not* a surveyor. Before he shifted the last load
of rock he had yanked the theodolite out of the ground,
not bothering to take off the head of the instrument, and
bundled it bodily into the landrover. You did not treat a

precision instrument like that, not if you were a surveyor.

She wondered, briefly, whether to tell the aunt but decided against it. The aunt would not believe her because she would not want to believe there was anything suspicious about 'that nice Mr Bollow'.

She slipped into the house unseen and shed her wet clothes. As she returned from her bath she saw Bollow hanging about in the hall, fidgeting and restless.

The telephone rang and Bollow snatched it before it could ring again.

'Yeah! Here!'

Cilla knelt once more on the upstairs landing. His voice was lowered but the house was silent except for the tick of the big old clock at the foot of the stairs and she could hear him, hoarse, on edge.

'Right . . . So it's on . . . You're sure . . . I will, I *swear* I will!' He set down the receiver and it rattled on its stand. His hand was shaking as he lifted it to wipe at his face.

Cilla stole away. Tired, she went early to bed. The wind moaned around the house and rain tapped softly at the window.

'It's on. . . .'

What was 'on'?

She fell asleep with the question and Bollow's sweating face revolving in her mind.

She woke in the night curled tense as a wound spring in the dark, listening. Someone moved in the passage outside her room, passed with the creak of a board and was gone. She knew it was Bollow.

The luminous face of her watch showed that it was six-thirty.

She padded from the bed to the window. Bollow drifted like a shadow across the yard to the garage, the figure unmistakable despite the covering darkness.

He slid back the garage doors and disappeared inside. A moment later his landrover nosed out with Bollow leaning in at the open front door with one hand on the wheel, shoving. It rolled steadily across the yard but when it reached the street and the steeper gradient it picked up speed. Bollow jumped in with startling agility and it rolled down the street and was lost to sight around a bend. Seconds later came, faintly, the mutter of its engine.

She scrambled hastily into jeans, anorak and boots, and crept downstairs through the silent house to the front door. It was unbolted. So Bollow had gone that way. She walked softly across the yard then ran down the street and out along the coast road.

2 The flight

In the aftermath of the storm the airport was a scattering
of lights across the plain, dark under an overcast sky. The
three men drifted like shadows through the darkness until
their leader halted on the edge of the light that spilled
from the airport building. All three wore the dark blue
coveralls of airport staff. The leader was a big man and
the light cast his shadow monstrous against the wall
behind him and glittered on his eyes.

He looked down at his watch and the faint light and
shadows made a sinister mask of his face. He moved on
silently, slipping back into the darkness with the others
padding at his heels.

In the airport building a pilot left the meteorological
office and paused while he carefully stowed away his
weather chart in his briefcase. He was fairly tall, a young
man but black-bearded. He walked across the hall and
passed through a door marked: STAFF ONLY. It led to a
short passage lined with doors that opened on to store-
rooms and cupboards, and went through to the rear of the
building. In the passage he met the three men in blue
coveralls.

After a minute the three men stepped from the far end of the passage on to the wet concrete at the rear of the building. There was a light over the door and they moved quickly away from it into the sheltering darkness and then halted. The big man carried the pilot's jacket and cap in one hand and he held up the jacket. One of the other men was about the height of the pilot – and black-bearded. He shrugged out of his coveralls. The trousers he wore underneath were dark blue like the pilot's jacket and cap that he put on. He felt at the beard and asked breathlessly, 'Is this thing all right, Stack?'

The big man answered coolly, 'It's perfect. It will come off easily enough when we want it to but not before. Stop worrying, Duggan.' And to the third man: 'Gurney. The briefcase.'

Gurney's mouth was twisted into a permanent foxy grin. He handed the briefcase to Duggan.

Stack said, 'I've talked you through it often enough. Just do as I told you.'

They stared out across the wet concrete to where a small, twin-engined aircraft stood on the edge of the light that washed out from an open hangar. The dark-uniformed figure of a security guard paced back and forth beside it.

The big man said, 'We're right on time. He's expecting you so don't keep him waiting. Go!'

Duggan strode off towards the aircraft. The other two sidled out into the darkness, heading for the distant runway that was marked with a highway of lights, but their heads were turned to watch the pilot.

As Duggan came up to the aircraft he called cheerfully, 'You're new!' The words implied that he was not new, that this was part of a familiar round to him. The words and the tone established him as being there of right.

The guard answered, 'The regular bloke got a call to say his wife was took ill so they sent me over from the main office instead.'

Duggan knew about the telephone call because he had made it. He said sympathetically, 'Poor old Johnny. Hope it isn't anything serious.'

And he had Johnny's name right. So when he showed the pilot's identity card and produced the manifest and the aircraft's papers from the briefcase the guard only glanced at them, checking cursorily, then handed them back.

Out in the darkness the two men paused to watch and saw the guard turn from the aircraft and walk back towards the airport building.

Gurney said softly, 'It's working, Stack!'

Stack answered flatly, 'Of course it's working. You've got the radio safe?' He did not take his eyes from the aircraft. The pilot had boarded it a minute ago.

Gurney held up the two-way radio swinging on its strap. 'Safe and sound, Stack, safe and sound.'

'Take care of it. We may need it. If anything happens to that radio you'll wish it had happened to you.'

Gurney flinched at the warning, knowing it was not an empty threat, and cradled the radio carefully in one arm.

Stack led the way again towards the runway.

The aircraft taxied along the dispersal path and out towards the runway. It halted at the runway's end with its engines running up, and Stack and Gurney ran out of the darkness across the rain-washed concrete and climbed in through the open door. Seconds later it rolled down the runway and lifted off into the overcast sky.

It was 6.45 a.m.

CILLA: 6.55 A.M.

The rock-piles loomed out of the dark and she squatted by one of them, catching her breath, listening and watching. After a moment she saw a dim glow, crept towards it, and found the landrover nosed into its hide in the clump of bushes. The dim glow came from inside it and now she could hear a faint humming. She crept in on it, looking for Bollow but not finding him. That was when she became afraid. Bollow with his false smile in her aunt's house, or plodding distantly around the rain-soaked field in the grey afternoon, was one thing. Bollow out here somewhere in the dark; that was another matter.

She jumped as the voice crackled from the landrover then stood with hands to her mouth and her heart thumping as she realised the voice came from a radio.

'*Hello, Rover! The bird has flown and we're on our way! Over!*' There was a pause while the set hummed quietly, then the voice came again: '*Hello, Rover! Do you read me? Over!*' The voice subsided again into the humming and did not come again.

Cilla edged out into the field, her nerves strung tight now, wanting to know where Bollow was, peering all around her. She checked and crouched ready to run as she made out the figure standing tall in the darkness – but it did not move. It took shape before her eyes as her breathing steadied, and she walked on to it. It was a tripod some two metres high with a cross-piece on the top of which were mounted three big lights like monster car headlights. Wires ran from them to a twelve-volt car battery resting under the tripod.

She turned to stare up the field and as she did so three lights appeared there. They were about two hundred metres away where Bollow had driven one of his stakes that afternoon. They were not in a tight group like those beside her but spread across the field with thirty or forty metres between the outside lights. They did not shine towards her but pointed white fingers at the night sky. Against their glow she saw the thick figure of Bollow waddling quickly back towards her.

She drifted towards the landrover, knowing that while she could see him against the lights he would not see her. She crouched by the clump of bushes, blending into its black hump as if she were part of it, and saw him by the tripod. The lights mounted there blazed out and she screwed up her eyes and lifted one hand to shield them against the glare. The lights were on for only a second, flooding over the field down to and beyond the other lights so their vertical beams were lost in that wave of light. Darkness returned and she was blind in it. When her vision returned Bollow, satisfied with his test, had returned to the landrover. He stood listening, his face turned up to the sky, then pulled his coat around him and climbed into the landrover. The door slammed, then the engine fired and settled down to a mutter.

Surely he wasn't leaving?

He was not. Cilla crouched for a full minute until the night chill sank into her and she shivered. It was then she realised that Bollow was running the engine and sitting in the cab with the heater going.

It would soon be morning. She stood up, and far over the mountains there was one great flash of lightning, one last belated effort of the storm. Now she knew what Bollow was up to. Not exactly of course; it might be smuggling or some sort of espionage but whatever it was she knew the purpose of the lights and their beckoning white fingers.

3 To the Devil's Gate

Andy was afraid of the mountain.

He was a boy with black hair that was always tousled where he thrust his fingers through it and big, dark, dreaming eyes. He was thirteen years old that autumn of the big storm but small for his age and thin. When the growing roar of the engines woke him he thought the sound was the thunder of the storm as it retreated over the mountains but the engines growled louder then clamoured overhead and receded. He stumbled through the darkness to stand at the window. With his nose against the glass that was cold with the rain sliding down outside, he saw the navigation lights of the aircraft against the last of the night. They winked, winked steady as a heartbeat but shrinking with distance.

The lightning came in one great jagged flash that stood in the sky and painted its picture on Andy's brain: the black background of the mountains with the deep V of the pass that was the Devil's Gate, and stark against that background the aircraft hung as if suspended from the lightning, and glittered blue-silver.

He recognised it.

The night swept in to hide it and the navigation lights no longer winked. He shivered as the chill clutched at his bare feet then his breathing checked as the flame blossomed high and far away in the sky. In a second it climbed from a glow to a soaring pillar then collapsed on itself, spreading outwards. The noise of the crash came down the valley like the far-off slamming of a door, final, but the flames were a long time dying.

The house was the only one in the valley and tucked away at the head of it, isolated. He was alone in it. His parents were away for the weekend and the twins, Matt and Karen who were his elders by a year, had gone to a disco party at a friend's house the evening before. Andy wanted no part of it and stayed home. Karen had telephoned late in the evening to say that the friend's father's car would not start and she and Matt would get a lift out in the morning. 'Will you be all right?'

' ''Course I will.'

Of course. He was a self-contained boy, given to dreaming but not concerned at spending the night alone.

He fumbled for his clothes and dragged them on with his eyes still on that red glow high on the mountain. With his shirt flapping he dragged the curtains across to hide that glow then switched on the light. In trousers and shirt and slippers he ran down the stairs to the telephone, only to find it dead. He was disappointed but not surprised. The storm had already put it out of action twice before.

He stood with the dead instrument in his hands, trying to think. He did not know what to do. He could walk the eight kilometres down the valley to the next house and tell them about the aircraft, but what about the waste of time?

His thoughts wandered. He was certain the aircraft was Mike Chapman's. He was a friend of the family who worked for a small air-freight firm and he had brought them a model of the aircraft he flew. It was in Andy's room. Mike sometimes diverged slightly from his route to fly over the house. Andy could see the crash in his mind's eye and the pilot stumbling away from the wreckage, just as in the film on television a week before. On the other side of the mountain there was only the sea.

He wished Matt and Karen were there. He was certain that if they were in his place they would do something and not just wait tamely for help.

He climbed the stairs and finished dressing, putting on his thick socks and sweater. He moved slowly at first but then his eyes fell on the model and he dressed hurriedly. He had never liked it up at the Devil's Gate, not from the time he was just a tot. It was always windy, always grim. But, still, he would leave a note and be off at first light.

CILLA: 7.30 A.M.

Cilla tensed as the radio's humming cut out and the voice came again, hard, metallic. A second later Bollow's voice answered it. Cilla crept in on the landrover and eased along its side until she was poised just short of the door. The side window was misty with condensation. The voice crackled harsh and now she could make out the words: '... you get up here. I've told Bergman. He'll go back to harbour and wait till we call him. Do you read me so far? Over!'

Bollow answered: 'I hear you. Over!'

'OK. The tiger's up here and I'll not let it go. If anybody gets in the way it's their bad luck. Now *move!* Over!'

Bollow answered, 'Moving now! Out!'

The door swung open as the landrover shot backwards, wheels spinning on the wet turf, Bollow holding the door open at arm's length and hanging out to see behind. The door swept up Cilla before she could move, threw her into the crook of Bollow's arm and after a split second of gaping shock he grabbed her.

She tried to pull away and nearly twisted from his grasp as the wet anorak slipped in his fingers but the landrover had halted, Bollow's other arm came out and he hauled her into the cab. She kicked and fought in wild terror, arms and legs flailing. Metal clanged, cloth ripped and glass smashed. Bollow wheezed and panted but his arms clamped more tightly around her, bit by bit, until she was curled on the seat of the landrover, legs trapped and arms held. He held her there with one hand and reached for the telephone handset of the radio only to find it on the floor with its spiral cable snapped. There was no light on the radio now, nor did it hum and there was a big dent on its front. He flicked switches, twiddled knobs and checked connections but without result. Finally he glowered at Cilla. 'Your fault, that!' He clipped her with his free hand so her head rang.

Through the ringing she heard him ask: 'What was you doing here?'

'Just looking.'

'At this time o' night? Don't come the comic wi' me!' He lifted his hand.

'I saw you yesterday and wondered what you were doing. So when I saw you go off tonight I came along to watch.'

'Ah? And what d'ye reckon?'

'Reckon? I don't know—' Then inspiration was born of

panic and she babbled, 'I thought you were going to photograph nocturnals, you know, foxes and things. I thought the lights must be for that.'

The free hand took her head and turned it so she faced him. She could not meet his eyes. It wasn't that she was not prepared to lie because she was frightened enough, but that same fear turned her eyes away. She heard herself stammering on: 'I'm sorry if I gave you a start. I didn't mean to. I've got to be getting back. My aunt's waiting for me. In fact she'll be coming for me, soon.'

And all the time Bollow shook his head, slowly. Now he said, 'You're a poor liar. And she won't. You went off yesterday without a word. She told me. She won't look for you. Nobody will.'

'She will!' Cilla was trying to convince herself.

'Shurrup!' Bollow leaned over the seat, fumbled in the back of the landrover and brought out a coil of light rope. He tied Cilla's hands behind her and the end he secured to a bracket behind the seat. He shoved her along the seat away from the wheel, started the landrover and swung it out of its hide. With headlights blazing it raced across the field and in minutes the tripod and the other lights had all been dismantled and stowed in the back of the landrover. Bollow wheezed back into the driving seat, pulled a map from his pocket and examined it by the light from a torch. One thick finger traced a route, lips moving, then he nodded with grudging satisfaction and muttered: 'Bad road and a long, slow ride.' And as he swung the landrover out on to the road: 'Right waste o' time *that* was.' His eyes slid across to rest on Cilla, little bright slits in the flat face. 'And you. Bad luck, you are. Or it's the tiger, it always was bad luck, the stories I could—' He stopped short and reached out to finger a medallion that swung like a charm from the dash. 'Good luck, that is. But we'll have to do something about you.' The eyes slid away from her and from the problem. He muttered, 'I'll leave that to the big man.'

Now he could not look at her and Cilla realised that he was afraid of the 'big man'. Or of what he might do.

They were driving away from the village and though she was a stranger there she knew they were driving into empty land, heading for where the mountains swept down to the coast. The heater breathed hotly beside her but fear chilled her.

MATT AND KAREN: 8.30 A.M.

The sun had been up for thirty minutes but the low cloud hid it as the car ground up the valley and stopped before the house with its engine running while Matt and Karen climbed out, then it turned and drove off.

Karen said, 'What's this?' She picked up the note from the table. Matt peered over her shoulder and so they read it.

Matt ran out into the road. 'Andy! *Andee!*' He cupped his hands around his mouth and bellowed the name at the mountain.

Karen brought their father's binoculars and they took it in turn to search the forested slopes, and then tried to probe the cloud and mist that veiled the Devil's Gate.

Matt muttered, 'Can't see him. Can't see any signs of a crash or an aircraft, either. Nothing.'

'Mike's plane is the only one that ever comes this way, and he *does* fly over the house.'

'Only in daylight. And every time he's phoned beforehand to tell us.'

Karen persisted, 'Whatever got Andy on to the mountain must have had a strong pull. You know how he is about that mountain.'

'I know.' Andy's secret fear was a secret only to himself. But Matt said, 'And I also know about his imagination, we all do.' He lowered the binoculars. 'And we all saw that film last week about the aircraft that crashed and *he* was hypnotised by it.'

He strode inside and put back the binoculars. 'Let's get properly dressed for it and then go and find him.'

Karen picked up the note. 'I'll add a line or two to this and leave it for Mrs Johnson.'

'We'll be back before Mrs Johnson gets here.'

'I know. But just in case.'

Mrs Johnson was a neighbour who drove over each evening to make them supper and see that they were all right. She would not arrive until after nightfall, soon after six in the evening, and Matt had no intention of being caught on the mountain at night. Just the same . . . 'OK. Better safe than sorry.'

Ten minutes later, long-legged and walking quickly, they started for the Devil's Gate.

CILLA: 10.00 A.M.

Cilla dozed and woke and dozed again as they wound slowly along the narrow roads, sometimes barely tracks. Her eyes tired from staring out at the rain. The flick-flack of the windscreen wipers and the roaring heater combined to relax her so she slipped again and again over the edge of consciousness into uneasy sleep.

When she finally woke they were driving along a road

that curled at the foot of hills. A glimpse of a watery, climbing sun through a gap in the scudding clouds told her it was mid-morning. On her left the mountains climbed, forested, peaks in the low clouds. The sea tossed on her right, wind sending spray driving from the breakers.

The road opened out into a cove and a cottage stood near the shore. It was washed white, with square windows picked out in black two above two. There was a stubby chimney but no smoke.

Bollow switched off the engine, took out his map and checked it, then looked at the cottage. The blank windows seemed like eyes, watching them. 'Back o' beyond,' he muttered. 'Know what they call this place? Hangman's Cove.' He touched his charm then reluctantly climbed down from the landrover, walked around and opened Cilla's door. 'We're going for a look-see.' He untied the rope from the bracket and twitched it. 'Out. And behave yourself, or else.'

Cilla climbed down stiffly. Her boots were full of feet and her neck creaked. She stumbled across the rough grass, rooted in sand, as Bollow pushed her ahead of him. At the cottage he peered in at a window then tried the door and found it locked. 'Empty.' He looked up. 'Just as well. Don't want no Nosey-Parkers.'

Cilla followed his gaze and saw the telephone wire that led from the roof of the cottage to the pole by the roadside. They stood there for a moment and Cilla looked around miserably. Two boats were upturned on the shingle, well clear of the high water mark drawn by weed and flotsam. A little jetty ran out into the water of the cove and the sea there was quiet though it still looked rough outside the mouth of the cove.

They returned to the landrover. Bollow retied the rope to the bracket, then reached over into the back and brought out a canvas bag. It held a huge thermos, cups and a parcel of sandwiches. He reached behind Cilla, took the rope from her wrists and tied it around her waist instead with the knot at her back.

Cilla took the cup of coffee he poured her, and the sandwich. The coffee was strong but it was hot and sweet and she sipped it gratefully. The sandwich was her aunt's bacon, thick and juicy. 'Thank you.'

'Wondered when you was going to say summat. Right little chatterbox you are, I don't think. And you don't need to look at me like that. Them sandwiches was all bought and paid for proper.' The smirk returned briefly. 'Couldn't have Auntie setting the law on me for her bill, could I?'

When they finished eating the clouds had lifted slightly, enough to show a gap cut deep in the crests, a pass into which the clouds seemed to fall to be thrust out like breath on the cold air. Bollow said, 'That's the place. No doubt about it.' He started the landrover and they trundled slowly along the road until they came to a track that led upwards. Bollow turned into it and said gloomily, 'An' where we're going, that cut in the mountains, know what it's called? The Devil's Gate.'

Cilla braced her legs against the landrover's jolting. The track had been meant for traffic in some far-off time and was wide enough for the landrover though steep and twisting. But the landrover knew its job and Bollow knew his and they climbed on and on towards the distant pass while Cilla, with her left hand, the one on the side hidden from Bollow, picked and worried at the knot in the small of her back.

4 The Devil's Gate

Andy climbed the last steep slope of the mountain below the Devil's Gate, a wasteland of thin turf and patches of long, spiky grass that bent before the wind, the green broken here and there by the grey tooth of an upthrusting rock. There was forest again in the Devil's Gate, a green belt of it masking the entrance. Andy halted at the edge of the open ground and looked up to the Gate. He told himself that he was resting before this last climb but he was not tired.

The mountains climbed steeply on either side of the Gate but their summits were hidden in cloud that tumbled down into the Gate to roll there, stirred gently by the wind, puffed out like breath. As if it breathed. Yes, very nasty, he thought.

But he had left the note to say he was going up to the Gate. It had not been bravado and he had to prove that. The aircraft was there – it had to be.

He started to climb again and as he drew closer he saw a stream ran out of the forest and at that point the trees and the ground on either side were blackened, charred. He walked on more slowly until his feet sank into spongy wet ash and there he halted again with the mist wisping around him as the Devil's Gate breathed on him.

The aircraft had struck here at the mouth of the stream so that the first trees on either hand had scythed off the wings with their engines and fuel tanks and these had burned and the trees with them. Nothing moved except the mist. There was no sound except for the wind's soft sighing. He stood on the threshold of the place he so disliked in that terrible silence and before him lay the evidence that this was no film, this was real.

He went on again, slowly, moving into the trees, working along the bank of the stream. He passed the wrecks of the wings that were knotted and twisted metal and the huge, shapeless lumps that had been the engines. He walked softly through a tunnel in the mist that gradually thinned before him and closed behind him. There was a greyness before him in the mist, of something that took slow shape as he walked on to it until it stood clear.

The fuselage of the aircraft had rammed on along the bed of the steam and had come to rest slewed across it. The fuselage was torn in long, jagged gashes, the door to the cabin was open and over all was that stillness. He kept on, until he stood at the door with a hand on its frame at either side and peered in.

His first glance was quick, the blink of an eye, wanting to get it over and done with. But he retained an impression of a pile of crates secured to the deck, beyond them two seats and beyond them the pilot's seat.

Was it empty?

He looked again, heart thumping now. There was no one . . . Then he was in, boots scraping and slipping on the deck as he went forward past the freight and stood by the pilot's seat. It was empty, the seat belt thrown aside. He sighed with relief, then he remembered the film and the pilot walking drunkenly, staggering, lost. Was he somewhere in the surrounding trees?

The thought sent him back along the aircraft and he saw the cage for the first time. It was secured to the deck like the rest of the freight. Its door was held fast by a big padlock but the bars themselves had been forced, ripped from their seatings and bent aside. The metal showed bright where it had been gouged as if bitten. And long scratches scarred the deck between the cage and the door. What had done that? What had the cage held, and more important, where was it now?

The thought gave him pause and he hesitated at the door a long time. Finally he stepped out and stood in the silence, peering about him at the mist. Now it was not the silence he feared but what might break it. So when he moved cautiously into the trees and called, it was softly in almost a whisper that was lost in the mist. But he moved and kept on moving, further into the trees and deeper into the Devil's Gate.

The forest thinned and then he left it behind but the clouds still rolled down and the mist still coiled. Now he moved between the high cliffs that climbed on either hand into those clouds. The walls gradually closed in on him until he felt he could stretch out his arms and touch them both. One wall was overhanging just above his head and dripped moisture like a roof. The floor of the bottleneck was littered and sometimes heaped with rock that had fallen from the cliffs so that walking was difficult and once he had to climb over a heap of it. The place was cold, dank, and the walls shut him in.

He ceased his calling and moved more quickly until he came out from the pass almost running. Below him lay forest again and he walked down to it, halting only once to peer at a patch of turf that was scarred and scoured as if a weight had been dragged across it.

He went on, but slowly again now, and when he was into the trees and the mist that moved in them he opened his mouth to call but did not. Instead he listened. He was out of the suffocating grip of those walls yet still he was uneasy. And that scarred turf? But he went on, deeper into the forest, listening, moving quietly.

Then he heard movement. He thought he heard a voice, muffled by the blanketing mist and distant but the movement was nearer. Something crashed through the forest towards him, closer and closer until he could hear its panting breath and the pad of its feet.

CILLA: 11.15 A.M.

They crawled up the last incline to where the track ended at the original reason for its existence. To their right lay a gully in which were scattered the derelict buildings of some old mine workings. At the far end of the gully lay the shaft, driven straight into the mountainside, its black mouth gaping at them. They were close under the pass and the mist coiled down from it like smoke. Bollow did not like it, his face showed it and he turned the landrover around to point down the track then hauled on the hand-brake. 'For a quick get-away and the quicker the better. Devil's Gate! What a name! What a place!'

He tapped the horn and its note barked flat against the mist, but a moment later a whistle came in reply from somewhere in the mist. Bollow sighed gustily. 'Thank God for *that*!' He jumped down from the landrover eagerly now, took two strides downhill and bent to wedge a rock under the landrover's front wheel. And Cilla, her thin wrists raw from the rub of the rope but free of it now, jumped down and ran.

Bollow was downhill so she ran uphill. She heard Bollow yell, snatched a glance behind her and saw him coming fast, but the mist was close and she could see the spectral shapes of trees in it. Before he could gain on her she was into the mist and swerving between the trees. Bollow yelled, 'Stack! She's coming up your way! Grab her! Stack!'

A voice from ahead of her crackled through the mist. '*Right*!' She swerved away from it and it came again. 'Hear that, Duggan? Gurney?'

Another voice replied, and another, and she could not place these. She ran on, breathing hard and heart thumping, head turning. The voices called around her and she thought they sounded more distantly but she ran on headlong. She plunged into a scattering of gorse and crashed through it, her feet padded on thin turf and skidded on exposed roots but she ran on. Until she ran head-on into the boy.

CILLA AND ANDY: 11.30 A.M.

He put up his hands to fend her off as she put up hers to save herself, and for a moment they staggered like wrestlers as he went back under the driving shock of her. In that first instant she realised he was scarcely taller than herself and that he was as frightened as she.

Cilla had done all the running but she found her voice first. 'He's after me!' Andy gaped at her as she gasped out her story of the airstrip Bollow prepared and the radio message that spoke of a tiger and called Bollow to the Devil's Gate. 'Somebody answered him, I got the chance to run and took it.'

Andy said, 'It crashed.'

It was Cilla's turn to stare. 'What?'

'You said it was an airstrip but this Bollow drove away, it was never used.'

'So?'

'Could he have got it ready for the 'plane that crashed up here?' And he told her about that.

And then a voice bellowed and there was a banging and crashing of someone beating through the forest.

Andy whispered, 'You said something about a tiger.'

'The one on the radio, he said it was up here.'

He told her about the cage.

They stood in a little clearing. The sounds of movement were coming closer but though there was undergrowth clothing the ground between and around a lot of the trees they did not seek its shelter. When they moved, going away from the crackling searching, driven before it, they went together and they watched the undergrowth.

They stayed ahead of the hunter but he drove them on until the forest ended and beyond was shaggy turf. There was still mist though the wind was moving it, breaking it now. As they paused before risking the open ground a figure moved before them, taking only shape without feature in the blurring mist but with the stature of a giant.

They shrank down.

The giant's voice came low, not shouting but carrying through the mist. 'Duggan? Gurney? Bollow?'

Cilla twitched at the name. Andy still clutched Cilla's

arm as he had pulled her down, and he could feel the muscles jump under his hand.

Voices called in reply: one from their right, another from their left, a third, wheezing, from behind.

The giant said: 'I heard them. Now they're still. Wait.'

They tried to breathe lightly. The giant stood like a rock and the other men were as still. Moisture dripped from the trees and the wind soughed and pushed at the mist. They knelt in tall grass in the corner of a crescent of bracken, tight against it and merging with it and safe unless one of the hunters stumbled on them – or the mist lifted. And that was why the giant waited. The wind was rolling up the mist, shredding it. It tore a rift and they had a glimpse of a falling hillside and some buildings below. The mist closed but the wind parted it again, and again. In seconds they would be crouching in the open.

'*Andy!*'

He jumped as the call came then gave an anguished groan as another voice took it up.

'*Andy!*'

5 Tiger!

Matt and Karen stopped as the mist was swept away by
the wind. They had seen the wrecked aircraft and passed
through the Devil's Gate. To their left a steep-sided
narrow gully led into the mountain and it held a cluster of
derelict buildings. Below the gully forest again swept
down the mountain, but before them and between the
gully and the forest on their right the ground was open. A
landrover was parked there with its nose pointed downhill. The shadow of a fault in the ground, like a trench,
ran from it to the arm of forest. They took in all this with
one turn of the head and forgot it. The man took their
eyes.

He was a big man, tall and with wide shoulders bulging
the blue coveralls he wore. He had a strong face that
might have been handsome except for the mouth that was
trapped too tight, and the eyes. The eyes glared but the
man stood easily, thumbs hooked in the hip pockets of the
coveralls, smiling, but the eyes stopped them dead.

Movement tugged at the edges of their vision and they
turned their heads and saw a bearded man in a blue uni-
form jacket with the badge of wings on his breast. He

stood close on their right hand. On their left was another man in blue coveralls, lips twisted in a permanent foxy grin. Behind them wheezed yet another who mopped at his wide face with a handkerchief and whose eyes shifted restlessly, ill at ease.

The big man asked, 'Who's Andy?' It was a question that came as an order and Matt heard himself answering, the words jerked out of him. He explained how they came to be searching for Andy, and finished: '— so we thought he must have come this way, looking for the pilot.' He stopped, looking at the man with wings on his jacket. 'Are you the pilot?'

The big man answered for him: 'That's right.'

Karen asked, 'Have you seen Andy?'

He shook his head.

She went on worriedly, not liking the look of these men, but with Andy on her mind, 'We must search. Andy—'

The big man said, 'Sit down.'

Matt started, 'We've got to find Andy. He—'

'I won't tell you again.'

They sank down and the big man stared over their heads. He said, 'And, Mr Bollow, what about the one you collected then let loose?'

Bollow wheezed out how Cilla had tricked him and broken his radio in her struggles to escape. 'So I don't know nothing 'cept what you told me last night – to come up here. What's been happening, Stack?'

Stack said, 'The radio I took in the 'plane last night can go in the landrover. And you want to know what happened? It went like a clock. We left the pilot tied up in a cupboard and took off with a certain start of half an hour at least. Duggan knew the route like the back of his hand; the radar was working a treat and he even got a couple of sights of the ground and he managed to spot a couple of landmarks both times that showed he was dead on course. In last night's weather that was practically a miracle.' He paused, then: 'He got one more sight of the ground and that was when it went bad on us. We were coming to the mountain when the lightning struck—'

Bollow broke in. 'Lightning!'

'That's what I said. One shaft of lightning that struck us and left us with a complete electrical failure and one or two other things besides. The 'plane didn't want to fly any more.'

Bollow muttered, 'Lightning. The tiger's curse.'

Stack jeered at him. 'Oh, shut up with that gypsy's warning.'

Bollow mumbled, 'All right. But there *is* a story about a curse and: "There's more things in heaven and earth . . ." ' His voice died away with Stack's eye on him.

Stack said deliberately, 'It was a natural accident, a chance in a million and it just happened to us. But Duggan held on and kept his nerve. He couldn't save the 'plane but he got us down without a scratch, *and* he knew exactly where we were. So I set up the radio, called you and Bergman and here we are.'

Bollow said, 'But the tiger? That's all right? You said it was up here.'

'It's in a big steel chest that was locked in a cage. We broke open the cage and humped the box this far but that's far enough.' Stack nodded towards the forest. 'Fetch it.'

Duggan and Gurney set off and Bollow said, 'I'll fix up the drill.'

'You do that.' Stack stayed, still standing relaxed, his eyes now on Matt and Karen.

Cilla and Andy heard every word and watched through the stems of the bracken. Then Duggan and Gurney strode towards them and almost walked on to them but Duggan said, 'No. Further this way.' The two men swerved away, pushed into a clump of bushes close by, and dragged out a steel box half a metre square and almost as deep. They dragged it down to where Stack waited.

Bollow started the landrover's engine and opened the bonnet. He carried a coil of electrical cable in one hand. The end of it went under the bonnet of the landrover and he paid out the coil as he came up. When he reached Stack he halted, puffing, attached a small electric drill to the cable and knelt down at the box. The drill whined as he went to work on the lock.

Ten minutes later the drill's whining ceased and Bollow threw back the lid of the box.

Stack bent and lifted something from the box. It was wrapped in black velvet and seemed heavy. He said softly, '*The Tiger of Bengal*,' and flipped open the cloth.

There was no sunlight; the mist had retreated but clouds still hung over the mountains. Yet still, in that grey light, it blazed. It was an effigy of a tiger, little longer than one of the big hands with which he held it, but the gang gaped at it. Even Stack was awed into continuing in that hushed voice, 'Solid gold and crusted with gem stones. A hundred thousand pounds worth of them and I'm only talking about the break-up value. As a unique work of art and a piece of history it's worth two million dollars and that's what it's insured for. Two million dollars.'

Silence. The breath was knocked out of all of them as they stared.

Stack broke the spell. He carefully replaced the cloth,

covering that blaze of colour, and there was a stirring, a
general sighing. Karen looked at the faces of the men and
saw them staring greedily at the *Tiger*. When she looked
at Stack his eyes were on her. His lips twitched as if he was
going to laugh but he said, 'Now we can afford it, a penny
for your thoughts.'

Karen licked her lips. 'How will you sell it?'

This time Stack laughed outright. 'Good question. And
it's a good answer. I won't.' He chuckled in good humour.
'I'll ransom it. The insurance company will pay – a
million at least.'

Bollow returned with the parcel of sandwiches and the
thermos under one arm, the cups hooked one on each
finger. In the other hand he held a stout cat-basket, with a
lid at one end that opened. Stack took the basket from
him, flipped open the lid and carefully placed the *Tiger*
inside. 'Appropriate! A cat-basket for a very special cat!'

He put the basket in the front of the landrover, returned and seized a sandwich and a cup of coffee. 'And as
for the curse, the *Tiger*'s been around for six hundred
years and passed through a lot of hands. In that time
somebody's bound to have bad luck.'

Karen privately agreed, but she saw that Bollow did
not.

About five metres away Andy eased back from the
bracken, moving deeper into the shelter of the forest. Cilla
went with him and after a few metres he halted and whispered to her: 'Down the mountain there's a cottage on the
coast.'

'I know. I passed it.'

'Right. There's a telephone there and I know where the
key is. We go there sometimes when the people who own it
come on holiday.'

'What about them?' Cilla motioned with her hand. 'Your brother and sister?'

'Matt and Karen?' They were silent a moment and then he said, 'What can we *do*?'

Cilla shook her head. 'You're right. We'll try for the 'phone.'

They started down through the forest, moving on hands and knees and at first tensing each time a leaf rustled or a branch creaked as they eased by. But the gang were relaxed and talking among themselves now. Gurney laughed to set teeth on edge. Cilla and Andy gained confidence with distance and moved faster, down through the right-hand arm of the forest until they came to the fault and slithered down its side to splash into water that lay ankle deep.

Cilla whispered, 'Hold on.' She was staring along the fault at the landrover. It had struck a chord of memory.

Andy asked, 'What is it?'

'Matt and Karen — we *might* be able to give them a chance. It would be a bit of a risk but not much. We could get back into the forest and away as quick as anything.'

'What are you talking about?' Andy asked it uneasily because he had a feeling this seemingly fragile girl was more reckless than he would care to be.

She told him. There was a risk but there *was* a chance. And there was Matt and Karen. He swallowed and nodded.

Cilla led the way along the trench until they were close to the landrover. She lifted her head cautiously then wormed out of the trench on her stomach and Andy followed her. The landrover hid them from the gang as Cilla eased out the rock from under the front wheel. She wriggled back to Andy then got to her feet but stayed crouched. 'I remember what he did. Take off the hand-brake and push.' Andy opened the door and leaned in. He was a long time on what Cilla thought was the work of a moment and she became impatient. But then he emerged. They shoved. The landrover rocked, settled. They set their feet more firmly and thrust together. The landrover rocked, the wheels turned – it was rolling.

Gurney wiped his mouth with the back of his hand. 'What about the other two?'

Stack swallowed. 'You mean the mysterious Andy and Bollow's little monster? They've a long way to go to reach anybody's house. Forget them. All we've got to do is get down to the cove.'

Bollow reached out to lay his hand on a dead branch. 'Touch wood.' Stack's grin vanished and Bellow whipped his hand away. But he muttered, 'Tempting providence, that is.'

Exasperated, Stack demanded, 'All right, you tell me: what can go wrong?'

Gurney said, ''*Ere*!' He sat bolt upright. ''*Ere*! The rover . . . !'

The wheels of the landrover were turning, slowly, but even as the gang scrambled to their feet it began to pick up speed and roll down the mountainside.

'Get it!' Stack shouted and ran downhill. The others pounded after him.

Andy fell into the trench behind Cilla and they scrambled, splashing, along it towards the forest as the yells rose above them. Andy was bent almost double, hands clasped around his middle and moving slowly. Feet pounded and as they looked behind they saw Stack hurdle the trench with Duggan close behind. Duggan saw them, checked in his stride, and his open mouth showed pink in his beard. 'Stack! They're—'

'I *saw* them!' Stack's bellow came back. 'Never mind them! *Get the rover!*'

Duggan ran on, Gurney and Bollow on his heels, and Cilla and Andy reached the forest.

Matt and Karen sat open-mouthed for a second as the gang started downhill, then Matt seized on the chance. '*Break*!' They were up and running. The Devil's Gate was above them but the gully and the derelict mine buildings were closer. Matt swerved towards them and Karen followed.

Cilla and Andy saw them go. Matt and Karen's flying figures drew them and they turned and ran uphill. Cilla glanced behind as she panted into the gully and saw that Andy had fallen behind. He was stooped with his hands around his middle, moving slowly, but he was coming. She ran on.

She was on a track that led straight to the open mouth of the mine. The buildings were scattered haphazardly to her right. She had lost the other two but knew they must be somewhere in the buildings and she turned off, pace slowing as she wound between them. There were tumble-down sheds with their roofs fallen in; a long, low building with some windows boarded, the others gaping where the boarding had sagged away; and furthest from the entrance to the gully was a two-storey house – or office, or store. The door hung from one hinge. She hesitated, getting her breath. The voice called softly, 'Up here.' She saw Matt's face at a window above her, Karen peeping over his shoulder. Cilla slipped through the gap past the hanging door. There was a flight of stairs, rickety and without a rail. She climbed them and the others met her at the top.

Karen asked, 'Andy? Is he with you?'

They were all breathing hard, partly from exertion, partly from excitement. Cilla nodded. 'Just behind me.'

They went back to the window.

'There he is!' Matt pointed and called, 'Andy!'

Andy's head looked out of one of the windows in the long, low building and at Matt's call he saw them and his face lit up. One hand came out of the window to wave, then head and hand disappeared.

Matt blew out a long breath. 'He's on his way.' Then: 'Where were you two? Do you know what's going on?'

And Karen said, 'We were lucky. The landrover ran away—' Something in Cilla's face stopped her.

Cilla said shyly, 'That was Andy and me.' She explained how they had overheard every word and set the landrover rolling.

Matt said, 'You've got your nerve! And Andy!'

They could hear Andy easing through the broken door below so they were all together now. That was a good feeling.

Matt said, 'Anyway, we should be all right now. That Stack said they didn't want you and Andy and they probably don't want *us*. They'll head on down the hill. All they want is to get away. Why should they chase us?'

Relief washed over them. They had been hunted and captured, all of them frightened, but they had come through it all and they were free. They had beaten Stack and his gang.

Andy's feet scraped on the stairs, his head appeared

and there he stopped. The three above him were laughing together. To Cilla, it seemed as though she had known Matt and Karen for years, not for about a minute. They laughed until Andy's expression registered on them; then the laughter faded away.

He said, 'I thought I could get a bit of our own back on *them*. It seemed like a good idea. But then I heard what you said just now about them not chasing us. . . .' His voice trailed away.

They stared at him, uncomprehending. Then he took another step and they saw his hands were clasped in front of him and his anorak sagged over them. He lowered his clasped hands and the sagging bulge followed them down until out from the anorak and into his hands slid the *Tiger of Bengal*.

6 'They'll chase us now!'

They stared in shocked silence until Matt strode forward and took it gently from Andy's drooping arms. He cast one quick glance around the room, saw a broken floorboard and lowered the *Tiger* into the hollow below. While it was out of sight it was not out of mind but the tension eased, slightly.

Andy said dully, 'They'll chase us now.'

Matt did not answer that because there was no need. Instead he said, 'It's not your fault. If we'd headed straight for the Devil's Gate and kept going we'd have got clean away *and* with the *Tiger* and that would really have spoilt their game. *I'm* the one who led the way here but it just seemed the right idea at the time.'

He moved to the window. 'I can't see anyone coming.'

'But they will,' said Karen. 'We ought to get out or anyway try while we have the chance.'

Matt did not answer for a moment. When he did his voice was low and he drew back from the window. 'Two of them are coming now. Duggan and the fat one, Bollow.'

They edged up to peer past him and saw the two at the

mouth of the gully. Duggan stood with hands on hips and Bollow shifted restlessly from one foot to the other. Both of them were staring intently into the gully, heads moving as they searched with their eyes. Then they moved forward, edging apart, and started to search the buildings. They started with the first shed, Bollow poking his head in at a window while Duggan stepped in through the door on the other side. Then they moved to the next. They were working steadily, thoroughly.

Matt whispered worriedly, 'No chance of hiding anywhere. They're really *looking*.' He paused then said tentatively, 'Suppose I made a run for it and drew them off, then the rest of you might slip away.'

Nobody liked that. Karen said, 'No,' and the others shook their heads.

Then Andy whispered excitedly, 'That long building hasn't any windows in the back.'

Matt peered at it where it lay to his left and between him and the searchers. 'I'm not surprised. It's backed close on to the wall of the gully. There's hardly a metre of space behind it.'

'So nobody can look in at a back window, they can only go in the front.'

Matt peered again and saw that the gap between the building and the side of the gully was a narrow passage choked with tall grass and taller weeds.

Bollow and Duggan were walking around another shed.

Matt said. 'We'll try it.'

He led them down the stairs. They could not use the door because they could have been seen. Instead they wriggled out of a rear window where a couple of boards had rotted and fallen, leaving a space. Matt went head first with Karen holding his legs and guiding them through so he did not kick the sides because they had to be silent. Any sound would carry along the gully. They could hear the two men's voices. Karen and Cilla followed in the same way and Andy brought up the rear, Matt leaning in to guide his legs.

They edged to the corner of the house and looked up the gully. They could not see the searchers but the long building was about ten metres away. They could still hear the men's voices, they seemed closer and Matt led on, trotting lightly across the open ground but tensed ready to run. The others followed in single file and they crouched against the long building. They were breathing hard again.

Matt whispered, 'Right down flat. Don't speak. Stop when I stop and *don't look*. But if I say run . . .'

He got down and wriggled into the passage behind the building and the jungle of grass and weeds closed around him. The others followed and Andy was last. He had hardly started to wriggle when Cilla, just ahead of him, stopped. He waited, his face pressed to the wet earth, one cheek against Cilla's boot. Footsteps echoed like drumbeats on the floor of the long building.

Matt hid his own face as Bollow stepped around the corner of the building to halt at the end of the passage. Matt held his breath. Their cover was barely adequate and that only because they weren't halfway along the rear of the building. If they had been a few metres closer to Bollow he must have seen them. If he entered the passage . . . .

Bollow took a pace and the grass rustled. His voice came, over-casual: 'Never seen anything alive up here, 'cept birds. Suppose there must be rats an' snakes an' things.'

Duggan's voice replied, hollow and irritable from inside the building. 'I suppose so.'

Andy felt Cilla's boot quiver against his face. He looked up and saw her staring back at him. He moved his head in a slow but definite negative and mouthed silently, 'No snakes!' The boot was still.

Duggan asked, 'What's at the back?'

'Nothing.' Bollow retreated hastily.

Duggan answered, 'Nobody here, but somebody has been; there's a print in the dirt here. We're getting warm. Come on.'

His boots beat out of the building, Bollow's footsteps crunched on broken stone and receded. Cilla moved and Andy followed.

They emerged from the passage and filed quickly between the sheds, keeping their cover between them and the two men until the mouth of the gully lay before them. They clustered together. They had got this far by helping each other and there was a bond between them now.

They trotted on out of the gully and the mountainside opened before them. And there was Gurney. He stood downhill, obviously acting as sentry. In the instant that they saw him and got a vague impression that the land-rover lay on its side, he saw them.

'*Here they are! Duggan! Bollow!*'

He started up towards them. Answering shouts came from far down the gully behind them and they ran. Matt led the way again and this time he headed straight for the Devil's Gate. There was no sentry. They ran through the belt of forest and into the Gate. Ahead of them it pinched in to the bottleneck between the steep walls. They were entering it when they heard the rumbling. Cilla took it for thunder but Matt skidded to a halt with them packed around him and stared upwards.

Stack stood at the top of the cliff thrusting at the loose rock that hung there. Rock was already pouring down in an avalanche and now under Stack's striving more broke free and thundered down, gaining momentum and growing in size as it collected rock and shale in its descent.

Matt shouted, 'Back!'

They turned and scrambled the way they had come, stumbling on the loose rock already there, as the avalanche rolled down and its roar blotted out every other sound. As the rumbling ceased they looked behind and at each other. The bottleneck was now impassable because rock filled it from wall to wall. Stack had slammed shut the Devil's Gate.

But worse, Andy was missing and they stared at the rock and felt sick.

Then they heard him. 'Help! Here! Look!' They saw a waving arm and a face behind it. They scrambled back to where he had fallen under the overhang and the rock had trapped him. It had left a narrow cave under the overhang and he was in there. There was a small hole through which his arm waved and that hand tugged at the rocks. They tore at them too. Cilla was conscious of his face, pale under the grime, and his lips shaking as he gasped, 'I'm all right.'

Then Karen cried out, '*Stack!*'

He was slipping and sliding down the cliff towards them like a great ape.

Andy's head and shoulders were out of the hole now and Matt seized him under the arms and strove to pull him free. Stack jumped on to the wall of rock.

'We've got to get away!' Karen cried.

Matt panted, 'I'm not leaving him!'

Cilla hovered. 'If we're all caught—'

Karen tugged at Matt's arm. Andy screwed his head around and saw Stack leaping down on them. 'I'm nearly out! Go on!'

Matt believed it and ran after the girls.

Andy believed it. He had only to pull himself out of the hole and run. But one boot jammed in the rocks, he kicked and twisted in rising panic, and pulled it free – as Stack landed beside him in a cascade of dust and falling rock.

Matt paused on the edge of the forest looking for Andy and saw Stack arrive. He should go back.

But then Duggan broke out of the forest, saw Matt and started for him. Matt's breath sobbed in his throat, and he fled.

Stack's face was streaked with dust and sweat and he wiped at it with one hand before reaching down. Andy shrank away but there was no escaping. The hands clamped on the shoulders of his anorak and yanked him from the hole like a cork from a bottle. Stack held Andy's shoulder with one hand and his chin with the other so he could not twist away from Stack's glare.

Stack stood for a moment, getting his breath, then said flatly, 'Where is it?'

Andy told him.

The girls kept together as they ran through the forest. That was instinctive. They could not think now. Events had piled one on the other too quickly and they just ran.

Karen was the faster and was two or three strides ahead of Cilla when they ran out of the forest and almost into the arms of Gurney. Karen swerved to her left away from him then found Bollow across her path, arms spread wide. She swerved again and the gully was ahead of her. Bollow herded her into it.

She found out what Cilla already knew, that the fat man was surprisingly quick on his feet. He could not gain on her as she fled along the gully but nor could she gain on him. There was no chance to hide. She tried, just once, to double back and he almost caught her, fingers clawing at her anorak before she turned and slipped from him again. He drove her down the gully until there was nowhere to go but the open mouth of the mine.

The roof was low over her head and when she was a dozen strides inside, the mouth of the mine was a grey half-moon behind her and the darkness ahead was pitchy. She had to slow to a walk. She heard Bollow's wheezing above her own panting breathing and saw him coming, bulking gross and black against the grey light. She backed away from him, stride for stride as he came on, his hands reaching out for her, his head pushed forward as he peered into the blackness.

She backed away until she took a stride and there was no ground beneath it and she fell.

Her shriek came up from the shaft, then was cut short in a splash. Bollow stood frozen, then cautiously went down on hands and knees and felt about until he found the edge of the shaft. He peered down into the darkness.

Cilla ran from Gurney. There was a narrow track through the forest and she took it and Gurney pounded after her. The track was steep and it twisted but while she could wend its twisting way better than Gurney, she was tired and he was longer in the leg. He gained on her. He was on her heels when the track came to the fault. They were deeper in the forest now and the fault was deeper, all of four metres, and two metres across. She had no time to set herself for the jump, leapt desperately and barely cleared the gap. A branch barred her way, she pushed past it and it sprang back behind her – into Gurney's face.

He had jumped the gap easily but the branch smacking into his face blinded him and set him back on his heels. He fell.

Cilla ran on with his yells in her ears.

Matt ran until his lungs laboured and then he halted and leaned against a tree to catch his breath, looking back for any pursuit but finding none. What to do? Should he go back and try to rescue Andy? But he was alone, he did not know where Cilla and Karen were or whether they, too, had been caught. No. His course was clear. He pushed away from the tree and started down through the forest, heading for the cove with its cottage and telephone.

He was careful now. There was no sense in tearing wildly down the mountainside and breaking a leg. He had to reach that telephone. Most of the time he moved through forest but there were stretches of open mountainside and before he crossed these he paused in the cover of the trees and carefully looked around for the gang.

Stack met Duggan at the overturned landrover, thrust Andy into his arms then went down into the gully and recovered the *Tiger of Bengal*. With that in his hands he went searching for the others.

His voice grated in the mine: 'Bollow?'

Bollow quavered, 'She's gone down this shaft.'

Stack came up behind him and knelt, peering. 'Who was it?'

'The tall girl.'

Stack stood up, stooped under the roof. He said heavily, 'Come on.'

'But we can't! We've got to—'

'You can't do anything. It might be thirty metres deep and you haven't even a rope!' He dragged Bollow away.

At the bottom of the shaft, movement sent a ripple across the black water.

They returned to the landrover where Duggan said, 'I'd better go and see what's up with Gurney.'

Stack looked around and Duggan said, 'Listen.'

They stood silent and heard the yell drift faintly from the forest. Duggan said, 'Maybe he's got one up a tree.'

Stack said, 'Give him a hand.' And to Bollow, 'You take a look at the rover.' He shoved him on his way then turned to Andy. Him he tied hand and foot. Then he carefully placed the *Tiger* in the basket and secured the lid with a small padlock. He tapped it, smiling secretly, then listened to Bollow's report. The smile slipped away.

Duggan returned, scowling, then said, 'I think he's broken a leg.'

Stack ground out, 'That's fine. Just what we wanted. Bollow tells me we've a busted wheel and you tell me Gurney's got a busted leg. How did that happen?' Duggan told him and Stack glared at Bollow. 'She's the one *you* brought along. *Tiger's* curse? The only bad luck we've got is you and Gurney.'

Stack went with Duggan and they carried in Gurney, his foxy smile gone and groaning or yelping at every jarring movement. They laid him on a blanket and started work on the landrover because they needed it for Gurney; they could not carry him all the way down the mountain. It had run downhill almost fifty metres before careering over a rock and sliding on its side. The three of them had to sweat with levers and the jack before they finally set it on its wheels. Bollow applied himself to changing the bent wheel and found one of the wheel bolts was bent and the nut could not be unscrewed. He had to cut it off with the drill before they could fit the spare wheel. Finally Gurney had to be lifted into the rear of the landrover and made as secure as possible against the downhill journey. It was three in the afternoon before they moved and Stack was raging and swearing vengeance.

7 Hangman's Cove

Matt came slowly down through the last of the forest and crouched at its edge, close by the road. His caution, his keeping to the cover of the forest all the way down the mountain had saved him from capture an hour or more before. The landrover had bumped down the track and he had watched it trundle slowly by as he crouched in the trees. But those precautions irked him. Unlike Andy, Matt had always walked where he willed on this mountain. Now Stack and his gang forced him to hide and skulk.

He hid now. He knew that to his left the road petered out at a derelict farm about two kilometres away. In the other direction there was no house for a long way. The cottage lay beyond the road, its two boats drawn up on the shore. The landrover was already on the road to his right and about a hundred metres away. It pointed away from him as if ready to go on down the road and the rear door was open. Duggan leaned there and Bollow paced restlessly. Matt could see Andy sitting in the back of the landrover and opposite him one man lay down with his head just showing at the tailboard. Gurney? It had to be because Stack was right inside, sitting beyond Andy; Matt could make out his massive figure in the blue coveralls. Stack had mentioned a radio, and – Bergman? So maybe he was in there talking to this Bergman on the radio.

Matt picked out his route. The road was easy. Just here it dipped and he could wriggle across out of sight of the gang. Beyond lay sand and a web of depressions, little shallow valleys worked by the wind. He got down on his belly and squirmed out on to the road. It was a good fifty metres to the cottage and he had to cover it all sliding flat along the ground but he did it in ten minutes.

In the shelter of the porch he stood up, dusted sand from his hands and reached up to the little niche where the key was hidden. It fitted and turned easily, the lock still oiled from the summer and he pushed open the door and stepped in. He saw the living-room of the cottage with its table at the centre and the armchairs by the fire-place at the rear. To his right there was a window and there the stairs climbed up and turned back from a landing to reach the upper floor. To his left was a window. It had been forced and stood open.

The door slammed shut behind him and he whirled to see Stack with his back set against it.

Matt stared, mouth open and wide-eyed and Stack laughed grimly. 'Saw Gurney and me in the rover, did you? Gurney's under a blanket in there but his coveralls are draped up over some gear. I'm here. Got in that way.' He nodded at the window that had been forced. 'It was obvious a local boy like you would know about this place and the 'phone and head for it.'

Matt jumped for the stairs. The open window was closer but had to be climbed through. If he could reach the bedroom and lock himself in. ... He had a split second of a start and the bedroom door was within reach of his clutching fingers when Stack's weight crashed into his back and flattened him on the upstairs landing. Matt was a big, strong boy and he struggled but Stack held him down, dragged a length of rope from the coveralls and growled: 'Brought this along specially for you!' He tied him hand and foot.

Matt shouted, 'Keep away! Stack's in here! Keep away!' In case Karen or Cilla were close by.

So Stack gagged him with a strip he tore from Matt's anorak as if it were paper. 'You won't shout through *that!* Not that it matters. There's only the one girl and she's probably still running.' He left Matt lying on the landing, tramped downstairs and opened the window at the foot of the stairs, right below Matt. This one looked towards the landrover and Stack thrust out his head and bellowed: 'Bollow! Fetch the rover over here!'

Matt thought dazedly, 'One girl?' Did that mean the gang had caught Karen – or Cilla? Was she in the land-rover with Andy? Whoever was free, he hoped Stack was right and she was still running, though she had a long, long way to go to reach help.

Matt might do better than that. He had not raced for the bedroom with escape in mind as escape had seemed impossible. Now he inched into the bedroom, working feet and elbows to slide himself along the floor. He had never been in the bedroom but he knew what was there, had heard of it in conversation during a visit to the cottage, and now he saw the bed, the little table beside it and on it the telephone extension, right by the door. His hands were tied behind him but he got to his knees, shuffled around to get his back to the table and was able to lift off the receiver and lay it on the table. With his head twisted over his shoulder so he could see what he was doing, he stuck out one finger and dialled nine-nine-nine.

Matt heard the landrover drive up and halt outside. Gurney's voice wailed fractiously, 'Leave that engine running and the heater on! I'm frozen in here.'

The engine throbbed on.

The telephone squawked: 'Which service, please, caller? Fire, police or ambulance?'

Matt mumbled through the gag: 'Bolice!'

'I'm sorry, caller. You are indistinct. Will you please speak clearly?'

Matt groaned, wild with frustration, tried to shout the word and only produced a meaningless mumble again.

Stack's voice below said: 'I'm going to call Bergman. Give me the mike.'

Matt was still for a second. Would it work? But he wasn't achieving anything like this. It was worth a try. He lifted the telephone and receiver down to the floor, collapsed beside them and wriggled out on to the landing, dragging the telephone and receiver with him.

'. . . caller. You must speak clearly. Which service, please? Is there anyone with you to make the call?'

That there was.

Stack stood below, fitting the headphones over his ears to blot out the engine's putter, holding the microphone in his hand. He said, 'Hello, Seaflight! Hello, Seaflight! This is Rover. Over!'

Matt worked his back to the banister rails, pushed the receiver through the rails and let it down on its cord so that it dangled behind Stack's head. The squawk came faintly, '. . . must speak clearly, please. Repeat your message once more . . .'

Stack said, 'Hello, Seaflight! You're loud and clear. Get a pencil and get this down. . . .' He lifted a map. 'We have the *Tiger*. We are at Hangman's Cove, grid reference. . . .' He spelled out the figures from the map. 'You come in now. I have one injured man but otherwise OK and all to plan now. Over.' He paused, obviously listening, then: 'Hello, Seaflight. OK. See you. Out.'

He pulled off the headphones and handed them and the microphone out of the window. Matt could just see Bollow take them – and Bollow's pointing finger. *'What's that?'*

Stack turned and found the receiver turning gently at the end of its cord only centimetres from his face. For a moment he gaped at it then his mouth shut like a trap, his fist closed around the receiver, snapped it loose and hurled it across the room. He crossed the room in two strides and grabbed the main, downstairs telephone from its place on a little desk in the corner. He ripped the cord out of the wall and hurled the instrument away. He strode past the window where Bollow stood peering, leapt up the stairs and seized Matt by the collar of his anorak. He dragged him down the stairs like that, legs trailing and bumping and dropped him on the floor in the middle of the room.

Bollow put his head in at the window and Duggan looked over his shoulder. Gurney whined from outside, 'What's going on?'

Stack's glare jerked Bollow back from the window and Stack's bellow shook the little room. 'We're *blown*! That's what! *He's* blown us!' He pointed one long, thick finger at Matt. 'He dialled that 'phone then let it down behind me while I was talking to Bergman. I don't need more than one guess as to *who* he dialled and they heard *every word I said to Bergman!*' He stood breathing heavily.

Bollow groaned, 'Ah! I *told* you it was bad luck. You wouldn't believe me, none of you. Now we've gotta run for it—'

Duggan said, 'You make me sick.' He looked at Stack. 'How long?'

Stack said quietly, battening down his rage now, 'Plenty of time. We're not running. Bergman will be here inside an hour.'

Bollow said, 'It'll be getting dark.'

'Doesn't matter. It'll be well and truly dark when the law finds this place with the distance they've got to come and that's all they'll find because we'll be away!' He was speaking very quietly now. 'But now we've got our pigeon here, all wrapped up. So we can put our feet up and eat. Bollow, you come in here and watch this bright lad. Me and Duggan will get out the grub and keep an eye open for Bergman.' His eyes were still on Matt, the finger pointing at him. 'But I won't forget you, bright lad.'

Cilla was still on the mountainside but heading for the cove and the telephone.

CILLA: 6 P.M.

It was dusk when Cilla moved through the forest and knelt with the road before her and beyond it the cottage crouched with those blank eyes of windows. The light was going fast now, the sun sinking somewhere behind the clouds still piled across the sky, but she could see the land-rover well enough. There was a narrow gap between it and the wall of the cottage, a gap already filled with shadow, but there was a dim light inside the landrover that filtered out from its rear door to silhouette a small figure. It sat in the gap with its back against the rear wheel of the landrover and every now and again it moved. There was a familiar lift and turn to the head. It was Andy.

She could not reach the telephone but, it seemed, there might be something she could do. She had no dreams of carrying out a daring rescue but if an opportunity offered she was there to take it, if the odds were right.

She tensed and shrank back into her cover as Stack stepped out from behind the landrover. He wiped his mouth with the back of his hand, lifted a cup and drank, then stared out to sea. She heard his voice, faintly, the words indistinguishable, but then he pointed and Duggan stepped out to stand beside him, both of them staring out to sea.

Cilla saw the launch ploughing in fast through the big waves with the spray bursting from her bow. Close to the mouth of the cove she slowed to a crawl and turned to cruise along the entrance to the cove, rolling in the rough sea. She edged across the mouth of the cove and then finally turned again to come in. A man stood in the bow with a long pole in his hands, using it to sound ahead of the launch as she inched in towards the cove. Cilla saw something thrown out from the launch, first to one side then the other, things that splashed in the sea and a moment later reappeared on the surface as the launch pulled ahead to leave them bobbing in her wash. She moved into the quieter waters of the cove and her engine bellowed briefly for a moment, echoing back from the headlands, then dropped to a mutter. She slid in towards the jetty like one more shadow in the dusk.

Stack and Duggan started down towards the jetty, Stack carrying the basket swinging from one hand. It was near dark. No one moved, no one was to be seen around the cottage – except Andy.

Gurney's voice bawled, complaining, 'What about me?'

Stack shouted back without turning or breaking his stride, 'You wait in the rover.'

'I can't do nothing else with this leg!'

'You can shut up! I'll see about your leg!' Stack strode on.

So Gurney was in the landrover and inactive now because of his leg! Had that happened when he fell into the trench? But Bollow? In the landrover, possibly mounting guard over Karen and Matt? Ah – she saw movement in the cottage.

So Gurney in the landrover, and Bollow in the cottage.

Long grass patched the sand between her and the cottage, and the ground was uneven so that the dusk made big pools of shadow. She could reach the landrover without being seen and return the same way. If at any time it looked dangerous she could turn back.

She hesitated and then suddenly she was on her feet and out of the sheltering forest, scurrying across the road and crouching double to blend with the shadows as she moved towards the landrover.

She was close up against it when she heard a movement inside that stopped her with one hand on the cold steel of its side. A groan came from inside but there was no more movement. She was breathing silently through parted lips now, and she knelt then lay full length and eased beneath the landrover. She edged across under the smell of grease and petrol with the salt tang of shingle under her face

until she came to the rear wheel. Andy started and his
head screwed around, his breath caught in his throat.

Cilla laid a finger to her lips and Andy nodded. His
hands were tied behind him to the wheel and she picked at
the knots in the darkness, edged forward again and Andy
also leaned forward so the little light that spilled down
from the landrover fell on the knots. Now that she could
see what she was doing her fingers had purpose and a
single, creaking movement overhead lent them speed. The
rope loosened, eased around Andy's wrists, then fell away.

Andy started to move, then froze as a voice said, ' 'Ere!'

It came from Bollow in the cottage. They saw just the
white moon face floating in the darkness at the cottage
window, the rest of him lost in the gloom. Cilla shrank
down behind Andy but she was ready to roll and run.

But Bollow said, ' 'Ere! Gurney! You there?'

Gurney's voice complained hollowly from the inside of
the landrover. ' 'Course I'm here. Can't go anywhere, can
I? If I move a muscle this leg hurts like it was coming off.
What do you want, anyway?'

Silence. Then Bollow said uneasily, 'It's lonely in here.'

'Lonely? You've got that perishing kid in there, haven't
you?'

'He don't say anything. Just lies there and watches me
all the time. Never takes his eyes off me. He don't help. I
don't like this place and I didn't like that place up in the
mountains. The Devil's Gate, Hangman's Cove, what sort
o' names are them for places?'

'Just names, just places—' A yelp from Gurney and he
went on: 'Now you made me forget and I moved! Look, I
don't know about him watching you but *you'd* better
watch *him*! Stack'll be back here any minute.'

Bollow's face hovered a moment longer. Then he said

vaguely, 'Yeah, well—' The voice trailed away and the face disappeared.

Stack'll be back here any minute.

Andy's head turned and he looked at Cilla. Then they were creeping along the narrow gap between the land-rover and cottage and around the front of the landrover. They were out of sight of Bollow in the cottage. They started back across the beach, heading for the road and the cover of the forest. Cilla led and she had to wait for Andy because he was stiff after sitting still for so long, but they reached the cover and flopped down into it.

For a few seconds they were silent, panting, eyes intent on the cottage and the jetty. Then Andy said hoarsely, 'Thanks.' Cilla did not answer and Andy went on, 'You heard what he said?'

'About watching? Who—?'

'Matt.' He told how Matt had been tricked by Stack into entering the trap of the cottage.

Cilla shivered. 'I was going to try to use the 'phone in there but I was too late.'

Andy glanced at her. 'If you'd been first then Stack would have got *you*.' A pause. 'But Matt got a message out.'

'How? You said Stack was in there.'

'That's right. But—' and he told how Stack had shouted to the gang that they were 'blown' and how Matt had done it.

Cilla whispered, 'Good old Matt!'

'Right.' Andy paused, then added worriedly, 'But he's in there.'

A silence again, that was broken by Cilla. 'Should we go down the road and look for help?'

'Where?'

Cilla shook her head. 'I don't know. Bollow brought me this way and I never saw a soul, not even a house for miles.'

'The police will be here before we could reach anyone.' Andy sighed. 'But the trouble is Stack is certain they'll be too late, that they've too far to come and he'll be away before them.' He paused again, then finished in a small voice, 'But he said he wouldn't forget Matt. I think he's going to take Matt with him.'

'Oh, no! But why? He's got the *Tiger*. I saw him carry the basket down to the boat.'

Andy muttered, 'Spite, I suppose. Because Matt spoiled his plan. Blow the *Tiger*. I'd swop the *Tiger* for Matt any day—' He stopped as the idea hit him, frightened and challenged him at the same time. 'If only he'd left it in the landrover again.'

'Why?'

He told her of the idea and saw her eyes widen. Then a rising scream of terror ripped from the cottage.

BERGMAN: 6.15 P.M.

When Stack and Duggan reached the jetty in the gathering dusk the launch was turning as she came abreast of the jetty. Then she eased in towards it so when the engine's mutter died away and she bumped gently, her bow pointed towards the sea. The man in the bow, dressed in oilskins, blue-chinned, jumped to the jetty with a mooring line and made it fast. The man at the wheel left it, moved aft and threw another line from the stern. Duggan caught it and made it fast.

It was a big, sea-going launch with a patch of deck

forward in the bow, then the roof of the cabin lifting up and filling most of the midships. Aft of the cabin was a well where the wheel was mounted and right aft was the housing of the big diesel engine. A dinghy was lashed on top of the cabin and another hung in davits over the stern. A big spotlight was mounted by the wheel.

Stack and Duggan stepped aboard. The man in the well was Bergman, bearded and broad. He wore stained, old jeans and a blue jersey. He pointed at the basket. 'What's that?'

Stack grinned. 'That's what it's all about.'

'That's it?'

Stack nodded. There was a companion beside the wheel and Stack went down the three steps, ducking under the overhang, and stood in the cabin. The others crowded down after him, Bergman flicked a switch and lights came on. There was a small desk close to the companion. It held a spread chart, held down by lead 'pigs', lumps of lead 30 centimetres long and 5 centimetres thick, at each corner. Piled by the chart were more 'pigs', coils of nylon line and a small buoy with a big clasp knife on top of it all. Each 'pig' had a hole through which a line could be threaded and tied. The buoy had a socket in which a small battery light could be clipped.

The air in the cabin was stuffy with the smell of fried food, coffee and diesel oil, and Duggan wrinkled his nose. 'It's a bit thick in here.'

'Bad weather outside.' Bergman unclipped the scuttles, swung them wide and air poured in through the open ports. 'We'll give it a few minutes' blow while we're here but you'll have to put up with the fug when we get to sea.'

Duggan grumbled, 'Took your time about coming in. Wandering up and down as if we had all night—'

Bergman turned cold eyes on him. 'This is a launch, not a 'plane or a car. It doesn't fly over the water nor drive on it, it swims in it. So it has to have water underneath it. There are sand bars running out from either side of this cove, the tide's ebbing and soon there won't be a foot o' water over them. So I had to find the channel and mark it with some o' them.' He nodded at the 'pigs', line and buoy heaped on the desk. 'Like I said, this isn't a 'plane and I'm not going to pile her up.'

Duggan reacted angrily. 'I didn't pile-up the aircraft! That was just bad luck.'

Bergman jabbed, 'Bad luck! You're worse than that Bollow. Seamen are supposed to be superstitious but some o' you lot—'

'That's enough.' Stack said it quietly but it cut Bergman short and Duggan swallowed the angry outburst that was on his tongue. Stack said, 'Duggan did a great job. So have you.' He made a space on the cluttered desk and set down the basket.

Bergman breathed heavily, greedily at his shoulder. 'Let's see it, then.'

'Later. Time for that.'

'Time?' Bergman was suddenly tense. 'How much time have we got now?'

'Enough so long as we don't waste it, so don't panic.' Bergman relaxed and Stack went on, 'Gurney hurt his leg, he can't walk and he's moaning about it all the time. Get your medical gear and see what you can do for him before we bring him down here.'

Bergman nodded. To the man in oilskins he said, 'Bose. While we're ashore you get out the dinghy from aft, take a couple of lights and mount them on those buoys. It'll be pitch dark when we leave here and I don't want to have to look for them with the spotlight in this sea.'

'Right.' Bose clumped up the companion and aft to the dinghy.

In the cabin, Bergman opened a locker and dragged out the attaché case that held his first-aid kit.

Duggan asked, 'Know much about doctoring?'

Bergman shrugged. 'Picked a bit up. Enough.'

'Enough? How do you know? You haven't seen him.'

Stack thrust him towards the companion. 'Because it'll have to be enough. Won't it? We're wasting time. Let's get a move—'

Then the scream came, faint with distance, and they ran.

MATT: STILL 6.15 P.M.

When Bollow turned away from the window he looked for Matt where he lay on the far side of the room and found Matt's eyes on him, watching.

Matt was stiff and sore and his nerves were on edge. Any elation he might have felt when his trick had succeeded, any feeling of triumph when Stack had bellowed that Matt had 'blown' them, had long since gone. Stack's promise had seen to that. Stack would not forget him. Matt lay on the floor of the cottage close to the window that Stack had forced. It still stood open, a pale square against the blackness of the cottage wall, giving a glimpse of an overcast, still threatening sky. The only light in the room came from the opposite window, a dim radiance shed by the light in the landrover outside. It was sufficient only to people the room with shadows through which Bollow prowled restlessly, soundlessly except for his soft wheezing.

Bollow prowled because he could not stay still. If he stood still then he knew he would hear the soft sounds in the house around him. He told himself they were only the sounds an old house will always make at night as the temperature drops and here and there a timber contracts and creaks. It did not help. He shifted uneasily, back and forth and around the cottage for minute after dragging minute.

But his prowling could not halt his thoughts and they returned again and again to the girl in the mine shaft, her cry that was suddenly cut off as she hit the water.

A sound came from near the window and Bollow checked and leaned forward, peering, but Matt lay still. Had the sound come from outside? Bollow raised his eyes.

She stood at the window, her hair wet-plastered to her skull and hanging damp to frame her face. The face was white, the faint light catching beads of moisture on the skin and the eyes were wide and stared horror-filled and horrifying.

For the space of a missed heart-beat Bollow returned that awful stare. Then he whimpered.

And then he screamed.

It racketed around the inside of the cottage and before its echoes had died away Bollow plunged through the door. The scream came again.

Andy and Cilla saw him burst from the cottage, sprawl headlong but scramble to his feet and run, still screaming. At first he ran towards the mountain but then he swerved across the shingle and made for the jetty. The others came running off the jetty to meet him and Stack grabbed Bollow by the front of his jacket and held him, shook him until his head rocked.

Karen swung through the window and eased the gag from Matt's mouth. His tongue was thick and the words came thickly. 'Do my hands first. We've got a minute. I heard them say they were going down to the launch.'

Karen tugged at the rope. 'I saw them. That's why I chanced it, I thought I might get to the 'phone.'

'It's smashed. What happened to Bollow?'

'I don't know. I looked in and there he was. It gave me the fright of my life but before I could run – well, you saw him.'

'And heard him.' Matt shook his head, bewildered. His hands were free. He rubbed at them but as Karen stooped to untie his feet he pushed her away hastily. 'I'll do that. They've got Andy tied up, too, outside at the back of the landrover just under the window. I heard them putting him there. If you poke your head out you'll see him. See if you can get him loose. Gurney's in the landrover but he can't move. They think he's broken his leg.'

Karen slipped across to the window like one more shadow, peeped out, craned out. Then her head turned and then she was running back. Matt was tearing the rope from his ankles. She dragged him to his feet and thrust him at the window.

Matt protested, 'Andy—?'

'Never mind Andy. I could see where he was because the ropes are lying there but *he's* gone.'

'Good old Andy!'

'They're running up from the beach! Stack's in front and he's *flying!*'

She had to help him through the window because he was near-crippled with stiffness. Once outside they hesitated but they could hear feet pounding up the shingle on the far side of the cottage. Matt knew he could not run and Karen said, 'I can't run. I ran most of the last stretch to get here to try for the 'phone.' Her face still ran with sweat, beads of moisture on the skin.

Matt said, 'Behind the boats.'

They limped across the shingle to the boats and dropped down behind the one further from the cottage, which was the smaller of the two.

Matt asked, 'What did you do? I mean, up there in the Devil's Gate when we were split up, what happened to you?'

Karen told him how Bollow had herded her into the mine and she had fallen down the shaft. She went on: 'I just remember falling over backwards – then nothing. I must have banged my head, in fact I know I did because I've got a bump here.' She felt at it tenderly. 'And I had a headache afterwards.' When she woke she had found herself half-sitting, half-lying on a heap of soft earth that had crumbled into a corner of the shaft. There was a half-metre of water in the bottom of the shaft but she had hardly wet her feet. The only light came greyly from the top of the shaft but it was sufficient for her to see that she had fallen about three metres. She was not very frightened because she was still woolly-headed. She stood up, felt around her and found that the shaft was timbered with cross-pieces around its sides set about a metre apart. She climbed out by using these.

Out in the air reaction caught up with her and she sat

down and cried. Then she dried her face and walked up
the gully. At its mouth she stopped and looked out. From
there she had seen the landrover and the gang working on
it so she retraced her steps and found a place where she
could climb out of the gully.

'I knew I couldn't reach the Devil's Gate without one
of them seeing me so I decided to head for the cottage and
the 'phone.'

Matt said, 'I was glad to see you. *Very* glad. And now I
think I know what got into Bollow. He thought you were
killed in that shaft, then when he saw you at the window
he thought you were a ghost!' He paused, then added
thoughtfully, 'Good job you didn't try it on Stack,
though. He's a different character altogether.'

Karen shook her head wearily. 'I didn't "try it on"
anyone. I just sneaked up to the cottage to see if I could get
to the 'phone. That window was open so I looked in. I got
the shock of my life when I saw Bollow. He was just
quicker than I was at starting to run.' She sighed. 'What
now?'

Matt did not know. It was a miserable hiding place and
the cottage was only forty metres away. They could not
run. There was Stack and Duggan – and how many men
had arrived aboard the launch?

What now? He knew what would happen if they just
waited behind the boat and Matt did not like it. He had
only just escaped.

8 The launch

Bollow ran into Stack as if he did not see him, as if he would run straight through him. Stack rocked to the collision but grabbed Bollow by his jacket and shook him. 'Cool off! Keep your head! Have you gone *crazy*?'

And as he shook him the words were shaken out of Bollow's rocking head. 'Her ... the shaft ... drowned ... hurt ... a ghost ... *ghost*. Looked in at me – *me* ... window.'

'Ghost? *Ghost*?' Stack threw him aside and raced for the cottage. He was a big man but he ran fast with long driving strides that sent the shingle flying. He passed the landrover, raced to the door of the cottage and charged in. There he halted, breathing heavily, just long enough to pick up the ropes from the floor then hurl them aside. He flashed his torch across the window and the floor then strode out to the landrover where Gurney kept up a continual plaintive calling: 'What's going on? Who is it? What's the matter? What was that shrieking? Horrible that was. What's going on? *Stack!* What's going *on* ...?'

Stack ignored him. He stooped by the rear wheel, picked up another length of rope and hurled that aside like the others. He pulled open the door of the landrover and tripped the light switches. The headlights came on at full beam and the cones of light blazed out across the grass and shingle and the road and lit up the trees beyond. It was a stark-lit, broad swathe slashed across the night but it showed no one.

Andy watched Duggan and the seaman leading Bollow towards the cottage. They seemed to be supporting him. His legs floundered under him. Andy took a deep breath and let it out. He whispered, 'What happened to *him*?'

Cilla shook her head. She said hesitantly, 'Well, they've gone.'

'Gone?'

'They've left the launch.'

Andy saw the point. 'That's right. It's a chance. We can't let them take Matt. . . .' But he hesitated, the chance thrust on him too soon so that he needed time to work up his courage.

Cilla did no answer but she was on her feet and moving and he followed at her heels as she ran lightly through the darkness well clear of the yellow circle of light from the cottage. They could see the gang milling around the landrover, crossing the white path cut by the headlights. Andy followed the flicking blonde mane that was like a pale flame in the darkness and wondered if it could be seen by the gang. Then he realised they would be blinded by the lights.

MATT AND KAREN: 6.35 P.M.

Matt and Karen saw the flash of a torch in the cottage, then Stack emerged. They crouched lower behind the boat as the lights of the landrover flooded across to the forest and voices were raised.

Matt whispered, 'They'll be organising a search.' He pounded softly with his fist on the boat. The light cut them off from the road like a door slammed in their faces. They could only retreat – but to where? His fist was still and he whispered again, 'I should have thought of it before! If they can get *in* that way then we can get *out!*'

Karen tore her eyes from the cottage to peer at him. She lay slumped against the boat, worn out. 'What do you mean?'

'You can't run, and anyway we can't get past that light. All right. Why don't we launch this boat, row out of the cove and around the headland?'

'Because I'm scared, that's why. It's rough out there, Matt.'

They started a whispered argument.

Stack glared from Bollow to Gurney lying in the land-rover. 'You two beauties.' He ground it out. 'Two grown men. Hard cases. *Hard?* I give you two kids all wrapped up, signed, sealed and delivered. You have to do nothing, *nothing* but *watch* them. You can't even do *that!*'

Gurney muttered, 'I couldn't do nothing, could I? Couldn't see him from up in here. . . .'

'He was right underneath you! You were sitting on top of him! You mean to say you didn't *hear* anything? No! You were too busy whining away about your leg. And you!' He stabbed a finger at Bollow, 'A ghost, you said. Ghost? It was *her*! No ghost! I don't know how she got out of that shaft but she did and when she got down here all she had to do was walk in and untie her brother and walk out again. While you were running around in circles howling your head off!'

Bollow's fat cheeks wobbled as he shook his head. 'I saw it. It was a—'

'*I've* seen the ropes. I've seen where she crawled in at the window and the two of them crawled out, and there are small wet footprints back and forth across the floor that couldn't ha' been made by anybody else *but* her. *Ghost!*'

Gurney said tentatively, 'Well, they can't have gone far.'

Stack glowered at him then bellowed, 'But *who's going after them?* You? Bollow?'

Matt and Karen huddled down as the echoes died away. '. . . *Who's going after them?*'

Matt whispered, 'You heard? We haven't any choice.' He saw her bite her lip and went on, 'We wouldn't be going far, just out of the cove, around the headland then back to the shore. That way we can reach the road behind them.' There was a note of desperation in his voice and a note of anger, too. He had been chased too far and frightened too much and now the reaction was starting to boil in him. He knew that Andy and Cilla were free, somewhere. He and Karen had only to keep out of the gang's clutches but he did not want merely to run away. He wanted to *do* something, to hit back.

Karen said, 'Well, if we have to. . . .'

He squeezed her arm. 'There's nothing to it, you'll see.'

She did not believe him, but she tried.

Stack got his temper under control. 'Searching would only be a waste of time. We might catch them and I'd like to get my hands on them because they know too much. But we haven't the time and where we're going they won't hurt us. Bergman, see to his leg and we'll get out of here.'

Bergman nodded, glanced inside the landrover then said, 'I can't see to do anything in there. Not much room either. Let's get him down and put him in front where the light is and then I'll sort him out.'

'Sort him out.' Gurney did not like the sound of it and started asking what it meant and protesting in advance. No one took any notice. They lifted him out of the landrover and laid him on a blanket in the blaze of the headlights.

Bergman made a quick examination. 'It feels like a break. We'll need a couple of splints.'

Stack bellowed in exasperation, '*So get them! Quick! We haven't got all night!*'

'. . . *Get them! Quick! We haven't got all night!*'

Matt hissed, 'They're after us! Come on!'

They rolled the boat over on to its keel, picked up the oars and dropped them in, then shoved it across the shingle and into the waters of the cove. Matt held the bow while Karen climbed in, then he pushed off, climbed in after her and past her to sit on the thwart amidships and pick up the oars. He turned the boat and pulled out into the darkness.

ANDY AND CILLA: 6.45 P.M.

The jetty was ancient, its thick timbers coated green with moss, slippery with rain and sea water, but solid. The lights from inside the cabin of the launch lit it up, but its underside was a shadowy cat's cradle of piles and crosstimbers. They crept underneath and worked their way out, crawling gingerly from one cross-tie to another, with steadying hands on the piles, bent double with the jetty right over their heads and the sea lapping black only a half-metre beneath their feet. The cross-ties were slimy with weed and dripped water and Andy thought absently that the tide was going out.

They stopped by the lighted ports in the hull and peered into the cabin. There were couches along both sides—

Andy hissed, '*There!*'

Right opposite them was a desk and the cat-basket stood on it.

Cilla whispered, 'I can see it.' The port was open and close to their faces. She lifted one hand and rested it on the port.

Andy shook his head. 'We can't get in through there.'

'No.' Cilla hesitated while they both stared at the basket. Then she said, 'We'll have to go aboard.'

'I suppose so.' Andy sounded doubtful. He was trying to find a way around it but there was none. He faced up to it. 'If we go together—'

'Yes.' Cilla put that in quickly. She was not going to be left on her own again.

So Andy shuffled carefully along under the jetty, Cilla following him until they reached the well of the launch. They could see over the side of the launch into the well and over its stern they could see the cottage and head-lights of the landrover, the men still moving there.

'Ready?' Andy looked at Cilla. She nodded and he gripped the side of the launch and rolled over it into the well. He crouched there, waiting until Cilla joined him.

Aft was the engine-housing, like a little cabin in its own

right in the stern. Twin davits also stood there but no boat hung from them. Forward was the wheel and compass, mounted on the bulkhead of the cabin; to the right of the wheel was the companion leading down into the cabin and its door was slid open.

They were both tense now, staring at each other. Then Andy said, 'I'll go down and get it. You watch for them coming back and call as soon as you see them. Stay here.'

He pulled her to the head of the companion but Cilla held him there. 'Wait. Look.'

A figure moved away from the light at the cottage, seen briefly as a silhouette against that light then blurring into a shadow barely darker than the darkness itself. It was lost as it crossed the hump of the cottage but the glimpse they had was enough. It was Stack.

He had glowered down at Gurney where he lay moaning and complaining on the blanket, his leg now rigid between the lashed splints, banister rails from the cottage. Bergman said, 'He's ready. Time we got back aboard and—'

'Wait. Those two—' Stack stopped.

Bergman pressed him, impatient to be away, 'You said it didn't matter about them. Which two, anyway?'

'The bright boy and his sister. They don't matter, but they're under my skin and itching. I want to check one thing. Wait.' And as Bergman opened his mouth to protest, Stack looked at him and said, 'Just wait.'

Bergman was silent. Stack turned and strode around the seaward side of the cottage and crossed the shingle until he stood by the boat that rested there. He stared down at the furrow in the sand where a keel had been dragged down to the water's edge, then raised his head to stare out at the sea. The blackness was pitch out there but the breaking waves were marking the sand bar in lines of silver luminescence. He stared, then chuckled deeply and whispered, 'Fly away, Peter, fly away, Paul. Come back, Peter, come back, Paul.' He laughed and he was still laughing when he returned to the others.

They looked from him to each other and finally Bergman ventured, 'What's so funny?'

Stack grinned at them savagely. 'You'll see pretty soon. You'll see.'

Andy and Cilla saw him walk back to the group and into the light and the laughter came to them faintly.

Cilla whispered, 'If we're going to, we'd better do it *now*!'

'I *am*!' Andy was rattled. The sight of the prowling figure of Stack and the sound of the laughter had raised the hair on the back of his neck. But he was committed. He wished he was not, that he had never suggested this. He said, 'You keep watch.'

'All *right*! But be *quick*!'

He started down the companion, a step at a time. No matter that it was empty. This was too much like entering the lion's den and he went with breath held and on tiptoe, eyes darting everywhere as soon as the cabin opened before him. The desk was close by the foot of the companion. Forward of the desk, couches ran along either side of the cabin and right forward it ended in a bulkhead.

The boat slipped quietly over the dark waters of the cove.

As Matt rowed they watched the cottage and the launch with its row of lit ports. They froze when the lights of the landrover flicked out and then a torch moved slowly, a bobbing cone of light, down towards the jetty.

Karen breathed, 'There's a boat.'

It slid in against the side of the launch and a man climbed from it. He started to haul the boat aft, tugging on the painter.

Andy stepped up to the desk. There was a chart on it, unrolled and held down at each end by a lead weight thirty centimetres long. There was a pile of more of these weights and a coil of nylon line with a big clasp knife on top of it, open and wickedly sharp. These things he saw only because they shared the desk with the basket. He reached out and lifted it, hefting the weight of it and then the fear left him. The cabin was empty and he had the *Tiger*. They had done it!

The launch rocked gently as something bumped and rubbed against the side.

Cilla crouched at the head of the companion, eyes fast on the group by the cottage, when the lights of the landrover went out. She blinked at the darkness, blinked again as a torch bobbed down the beach towards the jetty. Then she felt the bump and rub right alongside her. Instinctively she started to rise but froze when a big hand lifted above the side of the launch and clamped there. She could have run and she might have got away but she did not think of it. She might have shouted a warning to Andy but the sudden appearance of the clasping hand right by her face had struck her dumb. She did not think at all but only retreated instinctively from that hand and towards the only support she had. She backed down the companion, eyes fixed on the man who now stepped down into the well. He was blue-chinned and dressed in oilskins that dripped water on the deck. She was only a metre or so away from him and lit by the light in the cabin but his attention was all for the boat alongside. He started to lead it aft, pulling on the painter.

But now she was down in the cabin and turning to face Andy. His face was only bewildered, the excitement still with him as he clutched the basket but she saw the shock on his face as he read the warning on hers. Now both of them stood frozen as Bose's boots thumped on the deck.

Then a voice hailed faintly, 'All right, Bose?'

And the reply was shouted from the deck above. 'They're set dead to rights!'

They stared at each other. 'They're set dead to rights!' How could Stack have so cunningly baited and sprung this trap? It was uncanny. Cilla hissed, 'I don't believe it. He couldn't know. He wouldn't dare leave the *Tiger* if he thought we could get it.'

Her words came to Andy like cold water dashed in his face. Cilla was right, not even Stack with all his cunning—But they were trapped.

Feet trampled on the echoing boards of the jetty. The sound jerked Andy back to life and his hand reached out to seize the knife.

Gurney had a bad journey across the shingle. He swayed and bumped between the four men, one at each corner of the blanket. Bollow had one corner and lifted his share of the weight but he was good for nothing else. His fat cheeks shook continually and if Stack gave him the simplest order he only stared blankly, not listening, until Stack bellowed it at him, twice. Bollow, in his mind, was still running from the cottage.

They shuffled along the jetty and manoeuvred Gurney aboard into the well. Bose had hoisted the dinghy up on its davits so it hung broadside above the stern and now he was securing it. Bergman panted, 'Soon as you've made her fast, start the engine. Let's get out of here.' And to Stack, 'If you go below we'll pass Gurney down feet first.'

Stack stepped down into the cabin – and found Andy facing him, sick-faced, one hand clenched in a tight fist resting on the basket where it stood on the desk. Cilla stood a pace behind him by an open port-hole, her lower lip caught in her teeth. In his right hand Andy clutched a wicked-looking knife.

Matt rested on his oars. 'They were carrying Gurney. They're going to get away.'

He scowled at the launch and when Karen whispered, 'We can row back now,' he did not answer. She said it again and this time he shook his head.

He whispered in his turn and they argued, Matt set and stubborn and Karen weakening as the boat rocked on the little swell inside the cove and she looked out to where the sea broke in spray at the entrance to the cove.

She finally agreed and they headed for the mouth of the cove and the channel marked so plainly by the tiny, pricking lights. Beyond lay the sea and soon, too soon for Karen, it was bursting over the bow in sheets of spray that soaked them both and rolling under the boat from stem to stern so they soared and plunged as if on a huge see-saw.

They rode the see-saw.

Once Karen, crouched soaked and cold in the bow cried out, 'Matt! Can you hold her?'

Matt grated through clenched teeth, heaving at the oars, 'I can hold her if you can stick it. Just you be careful and *hold on*! Don't go over the side!'

The big waves rolled in and under them, burst over them and Matt strained at the oars knowing time was against them, that soon the launch would sail and take this course. But his mind was set as his teeth were set in this job and he would not let go. They stuck to it to the bitter end, till Matt had to let the oars slip from stiff fingers and aching arms and he dropped to his knees to bail with cupped hands as Karen was already doing.

9 Caught!

Stack stood very still for a moment that seemed to drag for hours while his expression changed from blank through disbelief to rage, until Bergman called: 'What's up? Come on, let's have Gurney below and get away out of this, Stack. What're we waiting for?'

'We have company.'

Stack's voice was quiet again, lips hardly moving in the set face, but the eyes burned at Andy and Cilla.

Bergman called again, 'What did you say?'

Stack answered, 'Two of our bad pennies have turned up again.' His eyes were on Andy and he slowly stretched out his hand. 'Don't try to be a bright boy, not like the other one, and don't do something stupid that I'll make you very sorry for.'

Stack's hand closed over Andy's, twisted the knife from his loose fingers then with a violent blow jammed it into the desk, pinning the chart. The desk shuddered, Bergman shouted from the well above them and when Stack let go of the knife it quivered as it stood with the blade half-buried in the wood. Stack pointed to the forward bulkhead and said one word: 'There.'

They shuffled back from him with hands pressed out behind them until they met the bulkhead, their backs were against it and they could go no further from that glare. They stayed there, pressed against the bulkhead, when Stack turned away.

Stack reached up and took Gurney's feet and he and the others lifted him down into the cabin and laid him on one of the couches. They gaped at Andy and Cilla. Even Gurney forgot about his leg for long enough to push up on to one elbow and point with the other hand. 'What're they doing here? He was one of them. She was the one as done my leg—'

Stack cut off his babbling. 'We know about them. And I can guess what they were doing here, or were trying to do.' He checked the lock on the cat-basket then lifted it, feeling the gently moving weight inside. 'But they hadn't enough time. They had enough to get on board and they could see us all up at the house but they didn't know about Bose. They got in all right but Bose came back before they could get out.'

A starter whirred, the diesel engine coughed, coughed again and burst into throbbing life; Andy felt it through his cold fingers on the bulkhead.

Stack said, 'You two can wait. Not for long but there's another little business I have to attend to first. Come on, Bergman.' He led the way up the companion, Bergman at his heels. His departure eased the tension like lifting a great hand from all of them. Duggan sat down on the couch opposite Gurney. Bollow joined him, wiping at his wet face with a dirty handkerchief.

Andy leaned weakly against the bulkhead, stole a glance at Cilla and found her eyes on him. They edged along the bulkhead until they stood close together. Their eyes went to the open ports. The launch was rocking gently now and they could feel a forward movement. Through the open ports they saw the piles of the jetty sliding past and then only blackness as the launch slid free of it.

Andy thought sickly that it had seemed such a good idea at the time but the luck had been with Stack and now ... Now the worst was still to come. And it was for nothing. Matt was already free. Cilla and Andy could have stayed in the forest, could have been there now.

On deck, Stack stood beside Bergman while Bose at the wheel conned the launch towards the mouth of the cove and the marked channel. Stack stood with one hand on the big spotlight and he muttered, 'Keep it slow. And keep your eyes skinned.'

He saw it first, a vague blur of movement and a white flash of spray against the dark water. He swung the spotlight, switched it on and steadied the beam. He said, 'All right, run alongside.'

Bose swung the launch to starboard and she ran down on the boat and rolled gently alongside as the engine slowed. The boat was half-full of water. Matt and Karen knelt in it, Karen bailing with an old can and Matt using his cupped hands. Or they had been bailing. The spotlight had caught them in the act and frozen them in it like statues except that they rocked with the motion of the boat. They panted with exertion and their eyes blinked and squinted in the light.

Bergman reached over the side with a boat-hook and drew the boat in. Stack leaned over beside him and dragged first Matt, then Karen over the side and into the well where they stood limply, dripping water on the deck. They were soaked.

Bergman asked, 'What about the boat?'

Stack was herding them down the companion ahead of him. He threw over his shoulder, 'Tie it on at the stern and tow it. We might need it later.' His chuckle rattled down the companion.

Bergman thrust the painter at Bose. 'You heard him.' He followed Stack and Bose left the wheel, the launch not under power and just rolling in the swell. He tugged the boat aft.

Matt and Karen stumbled down the companion and into the cabin, still blinking owlishly in the light. Duggan and Bollow were on their feet and Gurney had propped himself on one elbow again.

Stack enjoyed their surprise. He stood at the foot of the companion, stooped under the deck-head and grinned around at them with satisfaction. 'I saved these two as a little surprise. I saw they'd taken the boat. They thought they'd get away by sea but that was ignorance. Nobody knowing what that sea is like would try to get out of this cove in a cockleshell like that. Right?'

He shoved Matt back, one thick finger poking his chest, and Karen sidled along with him. Stack said again, 'Right?'

Matt and Karen fetched up against the bulkhead alongside Andy and Cilla. Matt scowled sullenly.

The finger prodded him yet again, and Stack repeated the monosyllabic question: '*Right?*'

There was a crack to it now.

Matt muttered, 'Yes.'

Stack nodded slowly, 'That's better. You're the bright boy, you can answer a question. At least you will for *me*!' He paused, then went on, rubbing it in. 'But you weren't too bright playing sailors. I knew what would happen. I knew you'd soon have a bellyful, and just about where and when we'd pick you up – providing you were still floating.'

His eyes went to Andy and Cilla. He nodded at them and said, 'And these two tried to be clever.' He backed away until he stood by the desk. 'They sneaked aboard to steal the *Tiger*.' He lifted the basket. 'But they were too slow.' He stroked the top of the basket with his free hand then set it down on the deck, wedging it in the space between the couch and the desk. 'We'll be at sea in a minute and we don't want *that* sliding all over the deck.'

He was smiling as he bent down but his face was hidden as he said the last words. When he straightened the smile had gone. His face was empty of expression. He said flatly, 'Now we're all together. No little tale-bearers running loose. Now we can tie up all the loose ends.'

Bergman shot a strained glance at him from where he crouched in the companion. 'Look, we don't want to do anything—'

'Shut up and get on with your job. I make the decisions around here.' He turned on Bergman, who took one look at that grim face and backed up the companion. Gurney sank back to lie staring at the deck above him, lips twisted as the leg pained him. Duggan stared out of a port.

None of them looked at Stack but Bollow muttered vaguely, 'Bad luck, that's what it is. Bad luck.'

As if the words had been a cue Bergman's voice shouted from the deck, *'There's a ship out to sea and closing the cove!'*

Stack spun around. *'How far?'*

Two kilometres. Maybe more.'

'You can slip her.'

It was a statement or an order, not a question.

Bergman answered, 'Easy! But close those ports! We want no lights!' And: 'Bose! Give her all she's got! Full ahead!'

Stack nodded at Bollow and Duggan and they started to close the scuttles and clamp them, shutting out the night, sealing the cabin.

Matt stiffened a little as the launch thrust forward, the engine bellowing. He whispered just loud enough for the others to hear: 'Stand still. Like me.' He lifted his hands and clasped them behind his head, leaning against the bulkhead. The other three stared at him numbly then mechanically followed his example.

Stack glared at Matt. 'What did you say? What're you doing?'

Bollow and Duggan, swaying unsteadily as they leaned awkwardly over the couches to secure the scuttles, turned their heads to look – and saw with shock and disbelief that Matt was glaring at Stack.

Stack could not believe it, either. He took a pace towards the children, his head out-thrust, peering.

Bergman eased the wheel a point, lining up the bow on the centre of the channel marked by the two lights. He had been right to set them. If they'd had to pick their way out now using the spotlight with that ship, whatever it was, coming in from the sea ...! As it was they would get clean away. The lights were sliding up on either beam as the launch hurled herself towards the channel and the open sea at roaring full-speed.

Then she struck.

She rode on to and into the sand-bank and from flying through the water she stopped dead as if she had hit a wall.

Chaos hit the cabin.

Stack, already moving forward, dived its length and slammed head-first into the corner. Bollow and Duggan were thrown to the deck in a tangle of arms and legs and Gurney shot from the couch to join them, splinted leg and all.

Matt and the other three leaning against the bulkhead were pressed against it but their hands saved their heads from whip-cracking against the timber. Reaction set them stumbling from it and Matt kept moving. 'Run for it!' He started for the companion with the others behind him.

Andy was a metre behind Karen. He saw Matt jump at the companion and Karen give a little skip as she followed him. Andy did not see its significance. Then his foot caught on the basket that had jerked free and out on to the deck. He fell over it and the steps of the companion rushed up at him. His head cracked against them, the lights whirled and the deck that had so suddenly become still once again heaved under him as he sprawled at the foot of the companion.

He lay on the deck. Only a second had passed because he was vaguely aware of Karen just leaving the companion above him. His head was still muzzy. He saw Cilla on hands and knees on the deck, crawling. She was caught like a kitten in a skein of wool, kicking at the tangle of line that had fallen from the desk and wrapped around her ankles.

He staggered back to her. He knelt beside her and tore at the line till it loosened and he could drag it from her and toss it aside. Then she was up and running for the companion.

He started after her but a hand clawed and caught at his anorak. It was Duggan. He was half-buried under Bollow and he looked dazed, but his hand fastened firm in the anorak and Andy could not pull free. Then his own hands found the zipper and ripped it down. He dragged out of the anorak and stumbled up the steps of the companion and out into the well. He looked for Matt, Karen, or Cilla but saw none of them. Instead there was Bose standing in the stern and leaning over it. A turn of the head showed Bergman right forward in the bow of the launch. He was sprawled on the deck with a torch in his hand, peering down its beam at the bow wedged on the sand-bank.

Andy was alone.

He knew what he had to do. He was not thinking clearly at all but instinct told him he had to get off the launch. He *had* to. He did not like the idea because while he was a good swimmer in a pool or swimming from a beach in safe weather, this was different. Here on the sand-bank the sea was a deal rougher than it was by the jetty, it was far from safe and the beach was a long way off. All the while he was tugging at the lacing of his boots but not liking the look of the sea. The second boot came off and he shed jeans and sweater. He crouched shivering at the side, eyes searching now for a lifebelt or something, anything that would help him. He saw Bergman was on one knee and climbing to his feet. Still he hesitated. Then Bose turned and faced forward, peering – and he heard a clattering movement in the cabin below and Stack's voice, slurred, indistinct but savage.

He went over the side as the shout came shrill.

The first bitter cold shock of the water took his breath away but he struck out. As he rose on the waves he caught glimpses of the shore, a long way off. He swam towards it, at first steadily, but then he looked over his shoulder and saw he was still abreast of the launch and remembered the tide. It was ebbing. He had forgotten about the tide but now it was sweeping out through the gap in the bar and carrying him out to sea.

He lunged forward in panic, thrashing raggedly, desperately and that wild effort drained away his strength. The sea crashed around him and he choked and spat and laboured on with leaden arms. Through the crashing he thought he heard the shrill cry again but his ears were full of water. Then the shadow swept down on him, lifted over him and hands came down to seize him.

There was a boat. Karen and Cilla leaned out over the bow, their faces frightened and close to his. The voice came shrill and it was Cilla. 'Matt! We can't – lift him!'

Then Matt was beside them, his weight on the bow bringing it down in the water, his hands also grabbing at Andy. Together they dragged him in to fall limp and gasping. He was aware of the boat's pitching and spray bursting over them and Matt and Karen scrambling back to the thwart amidships to seize an oar each. The boat spun around as they worked on the oars and it rode more easily. It drove towards the shore as they strained at the oars together. The tossing sea and the launch receded slowly behind them.

Cilla had pulled off her anorak and was holding Andy up while she pulled it on to his wet body. It was wonderfully warm.

Karen jerked out as she pulled at the oar, 'What happened – to you?'

Andy shook his head but he told them, teeth chattering.

Karen said, 'Bose was lying on the deck. We got into the boat but hung on to the stern of the launch. Cilla came and jumped down and said you were coming. But you didn't. Then Bose came after us and we had to shove off. Then we saw you jump.'

Andy shuddered. 'Bit of luck, that.' Then he remembered. 'Another bit of luck was them smashing the launch up like that.'

Karen shook her head. 'Luck be blowed. That was Matt's idea. We rowed out and moved the *second* of the buoys right round to the other side of the *first*. So they weren't marking the channel at all. See? And didn't it work!'

Cilla said, 'There's the jetty. Can you ease over towards it?'

Then the light stabbed out from the launch and pinned them in its beam.

Mat and Karen faltered then stopped rowing and the boat rose and fell slowly on the swell. The spotlight lit them up but they were too far away now for it to blind them. Squinting against the beam they could see that Bergman, staggering against the list of the launch as she heeled on the bank, had rigged a light on the mast the better to see the dinghy secured on top of the cabin. He was struggling to unlash it just as Bose was already lowering the other dinghy from the stern.

Matt said softly, 'They're going to leave her. She's hard and fast on a falling tide.'

Matt and Karen bent to the oars again. They could see that Stack was operating the spotlight.

On the launch Bergman paused to wipe sweat and spray from his face, squinted past Stack with a hand raised against the spotlight's glare and said, 'There are lights on the road.' There were three pairs of headlights sliding along the road to the cottage. Bergman reached down and lifted a pair of binoculars from where they hung by the wheel and set them to his eyes. He turned the knurled focusing adjustment and the blurred images of the cars became crystal clear. They had stopped now and he could see the men piling out of them only too clearly.

His knees gave way and he slumped down to sit on the edge of the cabin, feet dangling into the well, the binoculars loose on his knees. He said heavily, 'That's it. We're not going anywhere. Like you told the boy, nobody's going to sea in these cockleshells.'

Stack grabbed the binoculars, glared through them then threw them back at Bergman and blundered down the companion. He had to force his way past Bollow and Duggan who were hauling Gurney out into the well, Gurney one continual whine of complaint.

Bergman was using the binoculars again. He was not watching the police on the shore. He would see them soon enough. Vague, gloomy curiosity set him to watch the boat with its crew of youngsters bump against the jetty. They did not moor it and climb out straight away but manhandled it along the jetty. One of them, the small blonde girl, he could pick out that mane easily, was crouching to peer under the jetty.

He lowered the binoculars briefly as Stack snarled, 'Get me a hammer.' Stack carried the basket swinging heavily from one hand. He was glaring at Bose.

Bergman lifted the binoculars again. The boat was at rest now. The big boy and girl were out on the jetty, mooring the boat. The small girl was climbing out from under the jetty and up on to it. The small boy was—

Bose asked, 'What for? What're you going to do with a hammer?'

'Get me a *hammer*! I'm going to make a deal!'

Duggan said wearily, 'The police won't make a deal.'

'They will this time. Or explain how two million dollars' worth of *Tiger of Bengal* wound up as a mangled mass on the bottom of the sea. Now get me that hammer!'

Bergman lowered the binoculars and said huskily, 'Save your time,' and held out the binoculars. Stack snatched them then paused for a moment, for the first time uncertain, staring uneasily at Bergman where he slumped hopelessly.

Stack asked, 'What is it?'

Bergman only shook his head and pointed.

Stack set the binoculars to his eyes. He had to focus them again and he had to do it one-handed because he still held the basket, but the jetty swam into view, hazy then very clear.

The four of them were walking slowly out to the end of the jetty, the small, slight girl in the lead with the mane of blonde hair flying in the wind. She held in her arms something that sparked lights back at Stack to hurt his eyes.

He slowly lowered the glasses and let Bergman take them from his limp fingers. He rubbed at his face, peered at the basket and tested the lock, still disbelieving. He lifted the basket and shook it. But he had to believe the evidence of his eyes, what he had just seen through the binoculars. He slowly turned the basket over and felt the weight shift inside but then he saw the hole in the bottom. It was about fifteen centimetres across and hacked crudely as if with a knife and in terrible haste. He put in his hand and worked out a long lead 'pig'.

They walked slowly, wearily to the end of the jetty. Cilla sat down with her legs tucked underneath her and the *Tiger of Bengal* in her lap. The others settled around her in a little group.

Matt knew he was tired, very tired. His wrists trembled with the constant tugging at the oars, for he had rowed the boat single-handed all the time they had been moving the buoy, holding it against that awful sea. His shoulders were one huge ache.

Cilla had her back against his drawn-up knees. Karen leaned on one side of him, Andy on the other. All of them had legs like lead and shoulders slumped with weariness.

Karen had faced the sea with Matt and she had not failed him. She would remember that, was very glad, but she would forget the sea as soon as she could.

They watched the big launch beat in from the sea towards the cove, its searchlight sweeping, seeking and finding the launch fast aground on the bank. A signal lamp flickered from beside the searchlight and from the shore a policeman's torch blinked in reply.

Andy was sure he was not brave, and in a fleeting instant of perception sure that he would be afraid again, but certainly not of the mountain nor of the Devil's Gate. He had left that aboard the launch.

Cilla was one with them now, she knew that and was content. She was no longer alone.

They felt as much as heard the steady tramp of feet coming out along the jetty and waited for them, too dog-tired to move but close and warm together.

More Beaver Books

We hope you have enjoyed this Beaver Book. Here are some of the other titles:

Kidnap! Squib Lang, on holiday in France, is captured by mistake when a ruthless gang kidnaps a rich French boy. A tense and exciting thriller by Alan Evans, author of another Beaver paperback, *Running Scared*, which also features Squib. Illustrated by Peter Archer

The Mine Kid Kidnap A week's holiday in Wales for a party of London schoolchildren turns into a thrilling adventure, but when a girl is kidnapped the adventure becomes a real matter of life and death. An exciting and amusing story for readers of nine upwards by Eve Jennings

Wild Jack Set in the twenty-third century, this exciting story for older readers tells of a young City boy's capture by Wild Jack, the notorious Savage, and the decision it forces him to make. Written by John Christopher, author of the highly acclaimed 'Tripods' books, also published in Beavers

White Fang Jack London's great classic story about the life of a wild wolf dog at the time of the Gold Rush in the Yukon

These and many other Beavers are available from your local bookshop or newsagent, or can be ordered direct from: Hamlyn Paperback Cash Sales, PO Box 11, Falmouth, Cornwall TR10 9EN. Send a cheque or postal order, made payable to The Hamlyn Publishing Group, for the price of the book plus postage at the following rates:
UK: 30p for the first book, 15p for the second book, and 12p for each additional book ordered to a maximum charge of £1.29;
BFPO and EIRE: 30p for the first book, 15p for the second book plus 12p per copy for the next 7 books, thereafter 6p per book;
OVERSEAS: 50p for the first book and 15p for each extra book.

New Beavers are published every month and if you would like the *Beaver Bulletin*, which gives a complete list of books and prices, including new titles, send a large stamped addressed envelope to:

Beaver Bulletin
Hamlyn Paperbacks
Banda House
Cambridge Grove
Hammersmith
London W6 0LE

20304 2